CAPTURED BY THE LION

ALPHA CLAIMED

MILLY TAIDEN

CAPTURED BY THE LION

ALPHA CLAIMED

NEW YORK TIMES and USA TODAY
BESTSELLING AUTHOR
MILLY TAIDEN

ABOUT THE BOOK

Leigh Hale is on the run from a dangerous ex-boyfriend after she turned him into the police for running a Ponzi scheme. Now, she's back home and looking to start fresh. Of course, she doesn't expect to find the one man she's always been weak for at a coffee shop before she has a chance to shower or brush her hair.

Xander Caze has his hands full with his businesses and family. But when Leigh returns to town, he knows he needs to see her. He hadn't expected for adult Leigh to be so beautiful, sassy and full of life. Not only that, she's his mate. It boggles his mind to realize he's known her most of his life and just realized the same woman who proposed to him at five years old was meant to be his future wife.

Leigh's ex isn't the only problem in her life. No longer interested in going back to work at a big city, Leigh needs to find a new job. When danger comes calling from all sides, she'll get help from an unlikely person. Staying alive becomes a priority and Xander is doing his best to protect her. Too bad he might not get to her in time.

This book is a work of fiction. The names, characters, places, and incidents are fictitious or have been used fictitiously, and are not to be construed as real in any way. Any resemblance to persons, living or dead, actual events, locales, or organizations is entirely coincidental.

Published By
Latin Goddess Press
Winter Springs, FL 32708
http://millytaiden.com
Caught by the Lion

Edited by: Tina Winograd
Cover: Jacqueline Sweet

April 2020

❀ Created with Vellum

—For all my readers,

Keep romance alive!

CHAPTER ONE

Leigh drove through the night, only stopping for gas and making sure to keep to herself when she did. How had her life come to this? She flipped her coat's hood over her head and shrunk into the too big sweatshirt.

She should've known better. William was too good to be true. How many times had she said to herself, he was too nice, too perfect. Too damn honest. Honest? She snorted. God. The man was the biggest liar she'd ever met in her life.

Gripping the steering wheel hard kept her hands from shaking, something she really needed to control while driving. But seriously, she had to admit, she made the worst choices in men. Every man she'd ever dated had something wrong with him. It was just her luck that this one happened to be a thief involved with some massive Ponzi scheme.

She sucked in a ragged breath. Hold it together. It was hard. Leigh wasn't a rule breaker. She worked hard. Saved her money. Lived her life. So when she met William, she thought she'd run into a prize. After all, he told her he loved to be home and wasn't the partying type. Neither was Leigh. She'd always been the one to sit in the corner and feel awkward and uncomfortable.

Meeting William had been the worst mistake of her life. She choked on a sob. If only she could go back and change things. Fuck. How was she going to make it all right? How could she? She'd allowed him to destroy not only her life, but that of others.

When she got to her childhood home, it was already past midnight, but she was glad she made it and didn't deviate. William had no clue where she was. He knew her parents were dead, and her brother was overseas. She shoved her hair away from her face. God.

Turning onto her parent's street, she drove up the quiet road and then parked in front of their house. Her parents had built their house on a pretty decent piece of land. When she moved away for her job in New York, she'd been happy to leave the house to Kellan. But with his military job taking him all around the world, he was barely there anyway.

She sat in the car for a few minutes, watching the rain pelt the windshield. Air caught in her chest. No. She wasn't going to start crying now. This wasn't the time for that weak shit. She picked up her phone and opened the home security app and turned the alarms off. Swallowing back the sick sensation in her throat, she jumped out and ran to the trunk, got her suitcase and then dragged it to the front door.

The porch kept her from getting soaked. Inside the house, everything was quiet. Too quiet. She was used to the hustle and bustle of New York, not the cricket songs of a small town. Granted, Denali Ridge wasn't that small, but it was not New York.

Inside now, she locked the door and turned the security system back on. Paranoia had set in. What the hell would she do if William and his men followed her to Denali Ridge? What could she do? After all, she was the one who'd been stupid enough to tell on herself. She'd actually started asking questions.

Leigh dialed Kellan and nibbled on her lip while she waited for him to pick up.

"Leigh? What's wrong?" he asked immediately. It wasn't like her to call him in the middle of the night. It wasn't like her to call without asking him if he could talk first via messenger.

"I'm home." She sucked in a hard breath and tried to hold back the tears, but it was damn hard. "I fucked up, K. I mean so bad," she started blubbering.

"Shh, Leigh, it's okay. Whatever happened, we can figure it out," he said softly.

His tone only made her feel worse. Here he was trying to calm her down, and she knew that she'd gotten pulled into a fucking mess and had no idea how to get out of it. "I'm sorry," she choked. "I know you're busy and you have a lot going on, but I needed you to know I'm home." She gulped. "I'm...I'm scared."

"Why?" he asked seriously. "What happened? Did that guy do something to hurt you?"

She sniffled and shook her head. But he would. Once he realized she was on the run, he would go looking for her. "No. I... He didn't hurt me. But it didn't work out and he was..." she struggled to put the words together. "He's a thief, K. He's stealing people's money, and I feel sick. He took all my savings. Gone."

"It's going to be okay, Leigh. I'm so sorry I can't be there right now, sis," he said soothingly. "But I'll have Xander come and check on you."

Oh lord, not him. Xander Caze? She slapped a wet hand over her face and inhaled. "I don't need a sitter. I just need you to know I'm here. Okay?"

"I understand. I'm going to be home soon, Leigh. I promise," he said with determination. "Just lie low and call Xander if you need him."

"I already called the police back in New York. They should be opening up a case or investigating or whatever it is they do when someone's stealing people's money."

"Did someone actually complain? Like do they *know* he took their money?"

"He's an investment banker. He suggests investments to people, and they give their money to him." She squeezed her eyes shut and then let a choked sob out. "I was one of the people he took for a sucker."

"Sis, I can't talk more now, but I'll call you back tonight."

"It is tonight," she mumbled.

"I know, Leigh. Just hang in there. Trust me. I will help you through this."

"Okay," she said, her voice trembling and her body shaking. "I'm going to take a bath."

"Take a bath and while you're there order some Tomasino's Pizza. Eat and rest."

"Pizza sounds good. I'm going to order one," she sighed.

"You do that. I'll look into your guy."

She marched to her bedroom and kicked off her wet trainers. "He's not my guy. I didn't even know him. What I knew was a mirage. The guy was a fake."

"I know and I'm sorry, sis. Get some rest. We'll chat later. I love you, okay? You're not alone."

Her eyes filled with tears again and she sniffled. "Okay. I love you, too. Goodnight."

After the call ended, she slipped out of her wet clothes and tossed them in her laundry basket. She'd been glad she and Kellan had remodeled the house after her parents had passed away and created two master bedrooms so neither would have to fight over who got what room.

Each bedroom sat on either side of a long hallway. Her room was to the right. She looked up Tomasino's Pizza website and ordered online for delivery. She knew she was upset when she ordered more food than she was going to eat.

Steam rose from the rushing water. She watched her clawfoot tub fill with hot water. It was chilly outside, and the rain added to the cold, so the hot bath would help her relax. And think. She had to think of what to do now.

In a single moment, she'd realized she couldn't be there with William and act like she knew nothing. She couldn't continue to watch him steal from people while the police took their time doing an investigation.

At least she had told him she needed a break. Her excuse had been that she'd been working too hard and things were tough at work. But that was the least of it. Work had been fine. She was a banker. She knew how to handle everything from irate clients, to helping them open any necessary accounts. That's what she did. That's how she met William.

They'd been attending a business banking workshop and ended up working together during an exercise. He'd been so nice. So genuine. And she was a fucking sucker.

She wanted to slap herself upside the head. There had been signs. She had chosen not to look at them. William had immediately sucked her into his lies about how well his company was doing. He took her out on expensive dates. Showered her with gifts and attention. But more than anything, he brainwashed her into thinking if she didn't tell her clients about his company and the amazing return on the investments he was getting, she was doing them a disservice.

Leigh turned off the water and dumped in a handful of Epsom salt. She hoped the warm bath would help her clear her mind but also help her figure out what to do. Slipping into the hot water, she lowered herself until only her head was left out. Steam curled around her face. The porcelain at the base of her neck was still cold when she laid her head back and stretched her body under water.

Xander Caze. God. She hadn't seen Xander since she was like twelve years old. For a lot of her life, Xander had been there. Kellan's best friend since middle school. She had memories of them together since she learned to walk and talk.

When she was twelve, Xander went off to college and she hadn't seen him after that. He'd stopped visiting after they graduated. Both of them went into the military, and she never saw Xander again. She frowned. He might have been at her parents' funeral, but she didn't think so. He'd been all over the world doing top secret government stuff with Kellan. She'd been alone a lot after that.

Xander was the brother's hot best friend type. She'd been in love with him most of her life. Mainly with how beautiful he was. And that smile. He had a smile that made her smile. It was contagious. She sighed and sank deeper in the water, wiggling her toes.

She'd forgotten how gorgeous he was. Every little girl had a first love, and unbeknownst to him, Xander was hers. If only he knew she was "married" to him.

She grinned and rolled her eyes. He'd even played along when she was five or six. He'd held her hand and told her he took her as his wife and then kissed her hand and tickled her until she was crying from laughter.

Those were the days. Back then her biggest worry had been what toy she would play with. Once she'd become an adult, life had kicked her in the face a few times.

She thought back to when she'd gotten her first job offer in New York. Excited wasn't even the word. Ecstatic. She'd been over the moon happy. Kellan was in Paris, and she'd called him with the news that she was moving. She remembered how sad he'd been that she was leaving.

"I thought you would stay in town," he said.

She laughed. "You want me to stay in Denali Ridge, but you won't? That's not even fair, K."

"I guess not. I just always hoped that one day..."

"Listen, I'm still gonna come home and see you. And you're probably more often in New York than home anyway," she'd told him.

And he had been. A few times, they'd met up for dinner between his jobs. But she hadn't gone back to Denali Ridge until now. It was as if she'd been scared to return. To face the fact that this was the place she called home. But why? Why would she be afraid to return when nothing bad had ever happened here?

CHAPTER TWO

Xander Caze grabbed the shifter by the throat and squeezed. It was way too early in the fucking morning for this bullshit. "You think you're going to come here and intimidate my staff?"

The hyena shifter squeaked and gasped for air. "Fuck off."

Xander tossed him across the room. The guy's back hit a wall so hard, he left a dent in the wood. "Get him the fuck out of here. Take him out the back. I don't want his face seen on the floor. I don't deal with scum." He glared at the shifter. "Show your mug here again and I'm going to rip it off your head. Understand?"

The hyena glared at him, gasping for air. Julian

had two of his men remove the guy from Xander's office.

"Dude, angry much?" Julian asked with a chuckle.

"What? Would you rather I kill him for disrespecting Yudy? She's a fucking sweetheart and that jerkoff insulted her."

Julian raised his hands in surrender. "I get it. I'm just confused because you're usually a lot more chill. Like this kinda shit happens all the time. You and I both know that."

"Yeah. But tonight I'm feeling…antsy," he said. It was true. His lion was pacing restlessly under the skin. He wished he could know what was going on with the animal, but while they were one, he was a separate part of Xander.

"Well, chill the hell out before you kill one of the casino guests," Julian said with a laugh.

Xander's phone vibrated in his pocket. "K, what's up? Aren't you in Asia?"

"Yeah," Kellan, his best friend from childhood, said. "But I need your help."

"Is your current job too much?" Kellan and Xander had both been special ops, but now Xander was done with that part of his life. Kellan stayed. He loved the danger and the constant shooting.

"No. I've got this under control. I should be done here in a few weeks, but that's not my problem. Leigh is."

Xander's heart stopped. "What's wrong?"

"She's home. She's really upset. Apparently, the guy she was seeing is a scam artist and she might be in danger." There was worry in Kellan's voice.

"I'll take care of her," Xander said.

"You have no idea how much I appreciate that. I can't get away from this right now. I need her to be safe."

"Don't worry, bro. I've got her."

"Thanks. I'll call back and checkup, but I'm neck deep."

Xander knew all about that life so he understood why Kellan couldn't be there. "Go do your thing. I'll take care of her."

They ended the call and Xander continued staring at his phone. Leigh. How? The restlessness from his lion suddenly made sense. Leigh was back. Fuck.

"You got a look worse than when that shifter was in here," Julian said. "What happened?"

"My wife is home."

Julian reeled back and slapped a hand on his

chest. "You're kidding, right? When the hell did you get married? How did I miss that?"

He clenched his jaw. "She was five. I was twelve. We weren't actually married. But she was cute and something about her made me feel really protective of her."

"That's cute. And totally unlike you," Julian said. "Not the protective part. The fact a female got you to say I do, even at twelve is amazing."

"Shut up, you dumbass."

"I'm going to ignore you said that. So who's the wife?"

"She's Leigh Hale. Kellan's sister."

Julian dropped on a chair shaking his head. "Your best friend's sister? I don't see how you're going to survive this."

"I told you, she's not really my wife," he said. But when she'd asked him to marry her when they were kids, he'd actually considered it his duty to protect little Leigh. After all, that's what husbands did. When he went off to college, he forgot about the fake marriage. He hadn't forgotten Leigh, though. She was Kellan's sister and he'd always followed her life. From her first boyfriend to her move to New York.

She'd been a kid the last time he saw her.

Eleven or twelve. And it had been briefly. She'd taken up so many activities at school and after that she was never home when he went by. Little Leigh was busy trying everything.

And now she was home. Scared. That wouldn't do. He knew Leigh and Kellan had a tight relationship so if she was scared, there was real danger there.

"So is this fake wife your mate?" Julian asked, waggling his brows. "It would solve all your pride issues. Insta-mate. Your parents will get off your back about getting married. Your pride will get off your back about needing a female to lead with. Sounds pretty perfect to me."

"I don't know. The last time we actually spent time together she wasn't old enough to be acknowledged by my lion as anything other than a child."

"A child you wanted to protect," Julian said.

"Yes, but still just a child. How often do you recognize a child as a mate?"

Julian grimaced. "I've heard it's happened a handful of times, but I don't even know how. All the people I know have found their mates after they're in their teens or as adults."

Exactly. But he'd go over there and help Leigh.

She was Kellan's sister and Kellan was like a brother to Xander. He'd also help her because he felt the need to protect her from the moment he laid eyes on her as child. She was adorable with her bright red hair in pig tails and big green eyes smiling up at him.

He hadn't even seen a recent photo of her. He could contact a friend and pull one up from her license, but he didn't want to. He'd rather see her in person. The thought of seeing Leigh after all those years made his lion anxious. He wondered what the hell was wrong with the animal.

"Where are you going?" Julian asked as he headed to the door.

"I'm going to see Leigh."

Julian nodded. "Go get you a wife!"

CHAPTER THREE

Leigh winced at the bright sunlight streaming from her windows. She wasn't a morning person. She was an eternal night owl. Mornings weren't happening unless there was a ton of caffeine. She brushed her teeth, washed her face, and didn't even bother brushing her hair yet. Instead, she headed to the kitchen only to realize they were out of coffee. Fuck!

She grabbed her car keys and made a snap decision. Caffeine was more important than getting dressed. It was early anyway. Most people didn't get up until later in their sleepy little town. Not on weekends.

Driving down to the main street, she parked in

front of Ginger's Bakery. She frowned. It used to be Bun's N More. She wondered what happened. The bakery was empty. She grinned. Jackpot! She knew her townspeople were late sleepers on weekends.

"Oh my gosh," she heard someone squeal and blinked at the woman rushing out of the kitchen. "Leigh Hale, is that you?"

Ah, damn it. She wasn't ready to see people yet. Even if it was a good high school friend of hers. "It is. Ginger," she smiled and hugged the other woman who held her in a bear hug. "So good to see you."

"Girl, I'm so happy to see you! When did you get back? Oh, we have to talk. How in the world did I not know you were back? How's Kellan? Why are you here? Did you get married?" Ginger asked question after question without giving her a chance to answer.

She and Leigh had been pretty close in high school, but like most people once they graduated and went their separate ways, their communication had dwindled until it stopped altogether. She still got the occasional holiday email from Ginger wishing her happy holidays.

"Ginger," another customer said from behind

her, "how about you let her breathe and maybe she'll answer your questions."

Ginger let go of Leigh and then stared at her excitedly, trying to ignore the male whose voice had interrupted Ginger's way-too-happy morning questioning. "You're a sight for sore eyes."

Leigh closed her eyes and sighed. She wasn't interested in anything other than coffee. Why was this day not going the way it was supposed to?

"Ginger, get us a pot of coffee and two cups. I think Leigh needs caffeine to function."

Leigh turned to tell the man how grateful she was he'd put it into words because she was ten seconds from jumping over the counter and making her own damn coffee. But she stopped and felt the color drain from her face. No. This day couldn't have gotten worse. But it did.

"Xander," she cleared her throat and wanted to dig a hole in the ground and hide her head. "How, um, how are you?"

She kept hoping he was a mirage, but he wasn't. The fucker was real. All of him. Big body? Real. Gorgeous face? Real. Dressed to perfection? Real. That smile that made her forget who she was? Definitely real. Fuck. Fuck. Fuck!

"How about we hold off conversation until say,

the second cup?" He chuckled and grabbed her hand. A zing of electricity shot through her arm, and she yanked her hand away from him, staring at her fingers.

"Sorry," she mumbled and followed him to a table. She sat and dropped her face in her hands. She hadn't even brushed her hair. Why? How could the universe put Xander Caze, dressed like a freaking model, in her path on her first morning back?

"Are you okay?" he asked, his voice low and soft. Damn, that tone had grown deeper than she remembered.

"Uh, yeah," she raised her head and met his gaze. "I'm really sorry. I didn't expect to see anyone. I just wanted some coffee."

"I understand," he said, covering her hand on the table with his. "How does it feel to be back?"

Her gaze roamed his features, trying to age him from the way she remembered him. His eyes were still that hazel color that she'd been fascinated with all her childhood. When he smiled, they were greener. When he was angry, they were more yellow. There was a slight beard now. And damned if it wasn't the hottest thing she'd seen in her life.

"You look good," she said.

“Thank you,” he chuckled.

“Real good,” she stared at his mouth. She was going to hell. She should be thinking about taking a shower and brushing her hair, not about how sexy his beard was. Or wondering what the body looked like beneath the suit. Did he have tattoos?

Another chuckle and she realized she’d said basically the same thing to him twice. Fucking hell.

Ginger brought the pot of coffee with cream and sugar. Leigh filled a cup, added sufficient cream and sugar to make a candy addict happy and then gulped. She groaned and relaxed in her seat. Taking another sip of her coffee, she glanced at Xander over the brim of her cup.

He was busy watching her. Oh, boy. That look he was giving her wasn’t all that innocent.

“How are you doing, Xander?” she asked, emptying her first cup and filling it again.

“Ready to talk?”

She shrugged. “I’m not really a morning person.”

“That’s not the Leigh I remember. You used to be up in the wee hours ready to play and do everything.”

She choked on a laugh. “That was baby Leigh. Adult Leigh realized she prefers to sleep.” She sipped her coffee and met his gaze. "Sleep is good. I'm surprised you're here. I thought you would be out at one of your casinos." She frowned. "At least that's what Kellan said. That you stay in them a lot, managing and checking things."

He nodded. "It's true. I visit all the casinos and my family's businesses."

It was his turn to roam her face with his gaze. She felt the heat of it over her skin. Kissing her lips, caressing her jaw, and going up to her eyes.

"You've grown."

She grinned. "Can't stay a kid forever. I wish I could, but in the real world, people get older."

"That's not necessarily a bad thing," he told her.

She shrugged. "I don't know. I guess. Adult Leigh feels that she'd like a go at childhood again. It was a lot more fun than this adulthood crap."

"I see Leigh hasn't lost her spunk." He barked a laugh and she stared at his smile in fascination. The man was truly a work of art beautiful. His jawline. His lips. The eyes. Lord and that beard. He'd done good growing that beard.

"So what are you doing here? Just out for breakfast?"

He shook his head and stared her in the eyes. "I'm here for my wife."

CHAPTER FOUR

Leigh almost choked on her coffee. What did he say?

"Excuse me?" She glanced around. "I don't understand."

That wolfish grin was back on his lips. "I'm here for my wife."

She gaped at him. He couldn't mean— No. Did he? But how? Nope. Not possible. "What, um, what wife?"

"You."

Okay. She was going to need a lot more coffee than two cups to handle this. "What do you mean?" She blinked. "We aren't married."

That grin was starting to worry her. "Of course,

we are. You asked. I accepted. It's valid in the court of man."

She rolled her eyes. "I was five. Get over yourself." She snickered. "Besides, it's not like you saved yourself for me or anything like that," she stared at him. "I know the stories. You and Kellan and all the women you both dated. Come on."

He leaned into the table and she wanted to back away. The feeling of being caged in was suddenly all too real. "You're right. I guess the only way to fix this is to be completely faithful to you for the rest of my life from this moment on."

She blinked. Yeah. She was totally gonna need more coffee. Was he for real? "Did Kellan call you?"

"We spoke about an hour ago."

Now everything made sense. He was just using that childhood memory not to tell her that her brother had explained she'd fucked up and needed protection.

"Look, I know he probably said I'm going through some stuff," she shrugged, "but I'm okay. I'm handling things and I don't need a babysitter."

It was true. She would call that police detective. She'd gotten his number in New York, and he promised he'd follow up on what would happen.

"I understand you don't need a babysitter, but when there is a dangerous situation going on, having some protection is a smart thing," he told her, the smile gone from his face. "You know that. Having grown up with a lawyer father and a mother in the military, you know what I'm saying is true."

Fuck. She hated that it was. She'd been scared because she didn't have that protection in New York. That's why she'd come back to Denali Ridge. She'd been hoping to keep the danger at bay by going home.

"I know. I do understand what you're saying, and I'm going to be careful," she told him. "I promised Kellan I would be."

"Then what's stopping you from spending some time with me?"

She blinked. "What do you mean?"

The grin made a comeback. "I think you need another cup of coffee if you don't get what I mean. It's easy. I want to spend time with you."

"But why?"

He barked a laugh and she felt even more clueless.

"Because I want to. Do I need more reason than that?"

She raised her brows. "No. But I thought we agreed I don't need a babysitter," she said.

He nodded. "You don't. I just want to spend some time with you." He lifted her hand to his lips and kissed her palm. "With you."

"Oh," she said. But she still didn't believe he was genuinely interested in her. Because that would mean he found her attractive and then that could lead to all sorts of problems she definitely didn't need right at that moment.

Besides, he was her brother's best friend and totally hands-off. She wasn't going there. She'd barely come out of the last mistake alive. She wasn't ready to make another one just yet. And getting involved with Xander would be something she might not get over, ever.

"I guess that's okay," she told him. "I mean we're doing it now." She raised her cup and smiled. "Thanks for the coffee."

"What are your plans for the day?"

She snorted. "Plans? I was going to go home and get back to bed. I was working seventy-hour weeks and barely slept, so I'm going to take advantage of all the sleep now."

"So you're saying we may never see you awake again?" He chuckled.

With a nod, she drank more of her coffee. "There's a strong probability of that." She scrunched her nose. "I guess I'm going to clean the house. Looks like whoever does the lawn hasn't gotten to it, so I might do that, too."

"I'll come over and get that done for you. No need to worry about that," he said.

"You?" She stared at him, thunderstruck. "Um, okay."

"I'll bring lunch so no need to worry about that either."

Another surprise and she was nodding and standing. People were starting to come into the bakery, and she didn't need them to see her in her sweats, hair unbrushed, having coffee with Mr. Gorgeous.

She pulled out her credit card from her pocket, but he shook his head. "Please, allow me." Ginger came over when he made eye contact. "Add this to my account please, Ginger."

"You've got it, Xander." Ginger grinned at Leigh. "I'm sorry we didn't get a chance to catch up. Things get busy once it hits nine. Call me and we can hang out. Girls' night or something."

She smiled at Ginger. For real this time. "Thank

you, Ginger. It's really good seeing you. I'll call you."

He opened the door for her. "I'll walk you to your car."

"That's really sweet of you. Thank you." Why was he being so damn nice? She wanted him to be a jerk so it would be easy to push the temptation whispering at her ear away.

His perfect teeth made an appearance in another sinful grin. "I'm glad you're back, Leigh."

She cleared her throat. "Thanks. I'm glad I am, too." Though she wasn't going to tell him she was mentally stripping him way too many times. *Not happening, Leigh. He's off-limits. Perfectly off-limits.* "And you did say you're coming over to cut the lawn, right?" She frowned. "I didn't actually come up with that on my own?"

"I'll be there around one if that works for you."

She gave a jerky nod and got in her car. God help her. She was going to see Xander doing yard work. It didn't get much sexier than that. If he did her laundry and started cooking for her, she would have to hold him to that marriage deal. Marriage to Xander. That was her biggest childhood dream. She laughed at the thought. No way did he mean that.

CHAPTER FIVE

Xander watched Leigh drive off. Why in the world did his lion suddenly tell him she was his mate? It made no sense. Wouldn't he have known from the first moment that she was? He frowned and decided to pay his parents a visit. He needed to understand more about mating. With a shake of his head, he got into his SUV and headed out to their cabin retreat out by the Denali Ridge River.

The drive to his parents' took longer than usual due to the rain and a car accident along the way. Luckily, up by the river the sun was out, and the day was nice. He found his mom gardening, wearing a wide brim hat. The moment he pulled up, she raised her face and smiled at him. He watched her get up and dust her gloves off before taking them off.

"Xander!" she squealed. "My baby's here."

He chuckled and hugged her, letting her kiss him way too many times. "It's good to see you, Mom."

"Aw, honey," she sighed. "It's so good to see you." She searched his face for something. "What's wrong?"

He shook his head and laughed. "Why does something have to be wrong for me to be here?"

She raised curious brows at him. "Because you don't come all that often and I've noticed that when you do, it's because you need to ask for advice about something that's on your mind." She made a worried face. "I hope it's not pride related. Your father's out fishing with a friend."

"No. It's not pride related," he cleared his throat. "It's mate related."

Her eyes popped wide open. "Oh. We should go inside, and I'll make you breakfast."

"You really don't have to."

"How's steak and eggs sound?"

"Okay. You've twisted my arm."

She laughed and walked him to the house. "I'm really so happy you're here. I've missed you."

She sighed. "I know this is supposed to be our years to relax and all that nonsense, but I'm bored."

He sat at the kitchen table and watched her head to her bedroom. "You're not doing enough to keep busy?"

"I am," she yelled from the bedroom. "But it's the same thing all the time. There's only so much gardening and cooking a woman can do."

He guessed she was right. His father didn't seem to mind going hunting and fishing all the time. A moment later, his mom reappeared in different clothes. He watched her wash her hands and take out food from the fridge.

The cabin kitchen was his favorite part of that house. It was a chef's kitchen, with a center island that had an eating area on one side with stools, and the cooktop on the other, making it easy for the cook to look and speak to the person sitting across the way.

"So what is it you want to know about mating?" she asked, turning on the stove and heating a pan. She made quick work of pulling out rolls from the oven. "I made these earlier for your dad to take on his little fishing outing. Good thing he didn't take them all."

"If you meet someone as a kid, does your animal recognize that child as your mate?"

She glanced up from the stove and met his gaze. "Is this about Leigh?"

He stared at her with surprise. "How would you know that?"

She put a steak in the pan and put a second pan on for the eggs. "Leigh. Your best friend's little sister. The one who always made you feel protective of her."

"Yes. Leigh. Why are you saying it like that?"

"We don't have a lot of cases where a lion meets a human mate as a child. But I can tell you that from the shifters who've met their shifter mates as children, they don't really know that is their mate.

"All they know is that they feel a deep protective instinct for the other person." She flipped the steaks and cracked four eggs into the hot pan. "I guess since the animal isn't attracted to a child, the protective instinct is its way of ensuring the mate comes to no harm."

"What about the knowing? When does that happen?"

She slipped the steaks onto plates along with the eggs and carried them to the dining table. He took the bakery basket along with him and sat down. His mom put a plate in front of him and the other across from him and took a seat. "The actual mate recognition doesn't happen until both the lion and the human side are ready to acknowledge the attraction, both physical and emotional, toward the other person."

He ate and thought about what she said. If that was the case, he'd known all along that Leigh was his mate. His lion had replaced the usual mating recognition he had always known would happen for a deep sense of protection for her. He'd always been concerned for Leigh. From the moment he met her. At the time, he thought it was because she was an adorable little girl and he needed to watch out for her. Not because she might be his potential mate.

"Why didn't you say something to me before?" he asked her. "You obviously had an idea that she could be my mate."

She chewed on her food thoughtfully and then replied. "I guess because we had never had that happen to a pride alpha. You're the first. And I was worried that I was reading things wrong. My lioness told me that you and that little girl were meant to be, but I refused to say anything in case I was wrong. What if I put that in your head and your real mate came along later on?"

He nodded. "I can understand that. I guess I was always under the impression that I'd meet my mate as an adult. That I would know instantly. That I would be hit by the mate sense and that would be that."

She watched him and then cocked her head. "But didn't it happen that way now?"

"What do you mean?"

"I called your office earlier. Julian said you went to see Leigh." She raised her brows. "So, did it? Did you know instantly now that she's an adult? Were you hit by that need to mate, like your body will die if you don't spend every waking moment with her?"

He reared back in his seat. "Yes. It caught me off guard." He shook his head. "I hadn't seen her in so long. I knew the protective emotion well, but this..." he frowned. "This desperate need to have her as mine is new." He got up from the table and went to the fridge, pulling out a jug of orange juice and two glasses. He filled them both and handed one to his mom. "It was unexpected."

She grinned. "I'm sure. It's strange to suddenly realize you've found the one person you're willing to die for. The only person you ever want to spend your life with."

"Yes!" he admitted. "That's exactly it." He chuckled then. "You should've seen her. She looked a mess. Tired. Grumpy. Her hair all over the place with stained sweats. But I knew the minute our eyes met that I'd love that mess forever. No questions asked."

His mother dabbed at the corner of her eyes with her finger. "You're so precious, Xander. I hope convincing her is not the project I heard it is with humans."

Yeah. That. He knew she was reeling from a bad breakup. The thought of Leigh with another man pushed his lion to the surface. He wanted to rip apart any man that touched her and especially any man that hurt her.

"She just got back so I'll have to spend some time with her first. Let her get to know me."

She nodded. "Good idea, son. Make sure you romance the girl," she sighed. "Some men think they can just throw money at a woman and that's all she's interested in." She shrugged. "My favorite gifts from your father were always things he did or made for me. They were more special. More meaningful."

He'd have to keep that in mind. He definitely didn't want to be like everyone else. Not with Leigh. She deserved for him to go above and beyond for her. After all, she was his mate. There wasn't another woman out there for him. Now, all he needed was to convince her of that.

CHAPTER SIX

Leigh showered, changed into non-stained clothing and put some makeup on. Though she was trying hard to look like she hadn't tried hard, she didn't think it was working. She'd changed outfits like seven times and was glancing around her bedroom with a frown. It looked like a tornado had tossed everything all over the place.

Why was she thinking of Xander? She'd just left a lying thief who was probably out there looking for her. But did that matter? No. Her heart had gone back to her silly childhood crush on him and woken those feelings in a hurry. Though, now, it seemed they were a hell of a lot more potent. She'd never felt the desire she felt now for Xander. If she had, she might have embarrassed herself even more.

She settled on a pair of black leggings and a loose top. The other outfits weren't really practical for someone who was supposed to be cleaning the house. Yeah. She'd been so obsessed with what to wear and how to look for him that she had forgotten all about the cleaning.

Luckily, the sun was out, and he wouldn't have problems doing the lawn. She had prayed for the rain to stop her whole ride home. If it hadn't, he would've had to reschedule and that would have meant she didn't get to spend time with him while she was wide awake and looking human.

The sound of a car parking in the driveway made her yelp and toss all her clothes in her closet. Without hanging them up. She kicked and shoved until all she had to do was shut the door and keep the mess behind it.

Her heart tripped in her chest as she ran down the hall barefoot and hit her toe on a corner table. She screamed and hobbled to the front door, her eyes filling with tears and spewing every cuss word she knew and making up new ones along the way.

She unlocked the door but was still hopping on one foot when he walked in.

"Are you okay? What happened?"

She stared down at her toe. How was it not ripped off her foot when it hurt like it was?

"I hit my foot on the table at the end of the hall." She rubbed her hand on her toe. It was tender and would bruise, but it wasn't broken. "I'll be okay."

"Are you sure?"

She glanced up and almost swallowed her tongue. The foot drama had kept her from really seeing him when she opened the door. He wore a pair of jeans and a white T-shirt that had never looked that sexy on any man. "I'm, uh, sure."

What were they talking about?

He grinned and she definitely forgot how to breathe. "I brought lunch."

She gave him a once-over. From his days old beard down to his work boots. He sure had brought her lunch. "Thanks."

"Eat first or after?"

She bit her lip. "I don't want to sound like a fat ass, but I can always eat first." Unless they were talking sex. Then she could eat food after she ate him. Lord. Why was she thinking of eating him?

That was the last thing she needed. It would only lead to embarrassing thoughts. Of him and her. Naked. Doing things. Dirty things.

"Leigh?"

She blinked. "Hmm?"

He chuckled, showing gorgeous teeth and her hormones went haywire. She was in so much trouble. "I said let's eat."

Right. Yep. Lots of trouble. "We can go out back."

He carried the bag of food in one hand and the to-go drinks in the other. "I got you a lemonade. I hope you still like those."

She almost tripped on the patio entrance rug when she heard him say that. He remembered her favorite drink? How was that even possible? William had never made a point to memorize any of her favorites. She frowned. None of her exes had ever done that. They were too busy worrying about their preferences.

They sat at the outdoor dining area which was luckily under a cover and was nice and dry from the earlier rain.

"So what did you get us?" she asked, glancing at the plain brown bag.

"I went to visit my mom this morning, so I

picked up some fried chicken and the fixings at this great restaurant up there."

She frowned. "I don't think I've ever met your parents, have I?"

"No." He pulled out a bucket of chicken and sides along with paper plates and plastic utensils. "You were really young when Kellan and I graduated, so I don't think you were taken to a lot of the events we attended."

She picked up a drumstick and put it on her plate. "I remember I had the chicken pox when you guys graduated so I couldn't be there. I missed out on the party after, too."

He grinned and shook his head. "I'm sorry, but the party was lame anyway."

"I doubt it. You two used to have wild parties," she laughed. "I remember looking out the window and seeing you guys out here with a bunch of kids playing ball or in the pool."

"But you were doing your own thing," he told her and placed his hand over hers on the table. "I know you were. I remember your mom always telling us you had dance practice, or band, or soccer, or some sport." He shook his head. "They kept you busy."

She burst into giggles. "You have no idea. I

think they were tired of my energetic ass and were like let's have her try everything." Her poor parents. They had been older when they had Kellan so by the time she came along, they were not interested in running around after a little kid. They'd made sure she was entertained, but a lot of that time was spent on play dates and activities outside the house with a nanny to watch over her. "My mom was so sweet, but I think I was too much for her to handle."

He licked his lips. "You're a little firecracker."

And there went the bad thoughts flooding her mind. Bad Leigh. Bad. "I like to think I bring lots of drama and action into people's lives."

He barked a chuckle and she stared at him. That laugh always did her in. They ate and kept the mood light for a while.

"So what happened in New York?" he asked.

Well, there went the mood. "Nothing you have to worry about. I have a detective who's my contact there. I just dated a guy who was a slime ball and lied about who he really was. To me and to all the customers I sent his way."

"Has he threatened you?"

She gulped and drank from her lemonade. "No." That was technically true. He hadn't. "I overheard him threatening someone else. He told the guy he'd regret sticking his nose in his business." She let out a hard breath. That's really how she figured out what he was doing.

"He went out to visit a client and I went through his papers and saw the bank statements from multiple overseas accounts with all this money. And the paper trail was there. I took some photos and left." She snorted. "I'd already told him I needed a break. I felt like we weren't going in the same direction." She smiled sadly. "Clearly, I was going the non-felonious route while he bought himself a plane ticket out of Dodge."

"Get me your detective's name in New York. I'll have one of my guys check him out."

She shook her head. "Don't worry about it. As long as they do their investigation quietly, they can definitely catch him red-handed. I really don't have anything to worry about. I just got so scared being around a criminal, I didn't want to be there any longer. I really hope the police can get the clients their money back."

After lunch, she watched him head into the garage and she chose that time to pull some of the weeds that had started to come out around the edge of the pool pavers. She was sitting on a cushion, tugging weeds when the sound of the lawnmower came on. She glanced up and gaped. Xander was riding the lawnmower across their massive back yard, shirtless. She didn't know which deity to thank for that, so she sent a big smiley thank you to all of them.

Whoa, mama! Grown Xander was just as delicious looking as teen Xander had been. Only with a more developed body. He was strong, lean, and had that sun-kissed skin she wanted to lick all over.

She took twice the time to pull a single weed than necessary due to her lack of attention. Then she realized how she must look gawking and got up and went inside to ogle from the kitchen window like a normal person.

He'd done most of the yard while she stood at the kitchen sink and stared. She had problems. Big ones. Xander's gorgeous body was covered with a sheen of sweat and she couldn't stop her brain from telling her that's how he'd look from above her, pounding her out.

She was disgusted with herself. It was as if she hadn't had sex her entire life. But she had. Granted, none of her sexual partners had the sex appeal or even the sexual aura that Xander did.

They also hadn't done anything worth writing home about.

She shook her head thinking of how William told her he didn't give oral sex. That should have been her first clue there was something wrong with him. She knew damn well she wasn't going to last with a man that didn't want to eat her like his favorite dessert.

When he stopped the mower, she ran out and gave him a water bottle. "You're really going at it."

His eyes flashed gold. She'd always wondered about that color change but never bothered asking Kellan or even Xander.

"I want to," he said, holding her gaze trapped.

He wanted to? Fuck. That's not what she wanted to hear. No. Hands off. No dirty things allowed between them.

She cleared her throat and tore her gaze away to glance around the yard. "This looks wonderful. Seriously, thanks. I don't know when the person Kellan has hired comes to do it, but it really needed a trim."

"You're welcome," he said.

"I don't know how I can pay you for this. It was a big job," she smiled. Fuck a big job. She wanted to offer him a massage. Naked. Or some coffee. Also naked.

"Maybe you can pay me with dinner."

She snorted. "You don't want to eat my food. Your survival instincts might be put to the test."

"No," he laughed. "I mean we can go out to dinner. Maybe take a walk on the boardwalk."

"Oh." Like a date? Was he asking her on a date? Of course not. He was Kellan's friend. He probably just wanted to make sure she wasn't lonely. Be calm. She must be calm and stop talking to herself in her head. "Yeah. Sure."

"Tonight?"

She gulped. "I, uh, don't know—"

"Tomorrow. I can pick you up at seven." He glanced down at his watch. "I have to go to the office for a bit, but I'll call you later. I need to shower and change and check in with Julian."

She nodded, acting as if she knew who Julian was and wasn't totally freaking out because he was possibly taking her on a date. Maybe. It could just be a friendly gesture. Or he might want to get into her underwear as much as she wanted to throw them at him.

After he was gone, it took a good hour for her to get her brain into working order and stop daydreaming of him riding the lawnmower while sunrays bounced off his glistening skin like some sort of grass-cutting god.

The next problem was what to wear on her date. So what that it wasn't until tomorrow. She still needed to find the perfect outfit. She picked up the phone and called Ginger. Thinking about their friendship after she left the bakery, she realized that she'd been the one who'd grown distant. Ginger had called. She'd emailed. Hell, she'd even tried to visit. But Leigh had been so immersed in her new life that she'd pushed her away. Guilt ate at her insides.

Here was Ginger, still the sweet person she'd always been and still offering her the friendship she'd slowly pushed away long ago.

"Ginger's Bakery, this is Ginger."

"Hi, Ginger. It's Leigh Hale. Remember me? From—"

"Leigh!" Ginger squealed. "I'm so glad you called. After you left, I realized I didn't have your number and couldn't call you. I wanted to know if you wanted to hang out sometime."

She laughed at Ginger's enthusiasm. "Sure. Actually, are you really busy?"

"Right now? Nah. This is my break time. Why?"

"Um. It's best if I explain it in person. Do you remember where I live?"

"Everyone knows where you live. I'll come right over. Be there in ten."

True to her word, Ginger arrived ten minutes later, bouncing on her toes. "Hey!"

"Thanks so much for coming," Leigh said. "Come in."

They went to her room and she turned to Ginger. "Before we go any farther, I want to apologize."

Ginger frowned. "What for?"

"I was a shitty friend, wasn't I?" She shook her head. "I'm sorry. You know after I saw you this morning, I remembered how you'd tried to keep our friendship going even after I'd moved, but I was so involved in being in New York that I slowly stopped all communication." She grabbed Ginger's hands and squeezed. "I am truly sorry for that. You were always such a great friend. I should never have pushed you away the way I did."

Ginger blinked back tears and squeezed her hands back. "That's the sweetest apology I've ever gotten," she sniffled. "But you don't need to feel so bad. I had my own stuff going on, too. I knew you were living a new life. We grew up." She grinned.

"Now you're back and this is a second chance to be better friends."

She nodded. Ginger deserved a better friend this time around. "Thank you, Ginger."

Ginger cleared her throat. "Now tell me what's going on. Why did I have to rush over here?"

"I think I'm going on a date but I'm not sure."

Ginger raised her brows. "Wow. Okay. Do you want this to be a date?"

She frowned. "Yes. I…" she let out a loud sigh, "I shouldn't be dating. I just got out of a crappy relationship like four days ago." She met Ginger's gaze. "But I've wanted Xander my whole life."

Ginger blinked. "Xander? You're going out with him? Yeah. You definitely want that to be a date."

"I know," she groaned and threw herself on the bed. "This is insane. I feel like an awkward teenager again." She growled. "I hated that stage of my life. I'm not trying to relive it, damn it!"

Ginger patted her leg and nodded. "I know. I've been in some shitty relationships myself, so I totally get where you're coming from."

"So I don't know what to wear. Do I wear date clothes or hanging out clothes?"

Fuck, why did this have to be so hard?

"Wait. What exactly did he say to you?"

"He cut my grass." She shook her head and laughed at Ginger's smirk. "Not that grass, you perv."

"Yeah, okay. Don't tell me you didn't wish it was that grass."

Maybe. Yeah, okay. "He then suggested I pay him by going to dinner with him. So is it a date or not?"

Ginger burst into a fit of giggles. She stopped when she was breathless and fanned her bright red face. "Girl, this is so a date. Xander doesn't trim grass, of any kind, for anybody other than his mom."

Ginger frowned. "He's a billionaire. He doesn't do housework. He doesn't have to. The fact he did your lawn and then asked you to dinner speaks of his desire to spend time with you. And to do something kind for you." She glanced at her up and down.

"You definitely want date clothes. The type you wear when you know you're gonna give it up." She raised a hand. "Don't bother denying it. You're gonna get laid and it's gonna be out of your wildest dreams. I've heard things. Let's hope they're true."

She sat up, her eyes wide. "What did you hear?"

"That he's an animal in bed."

A shudder raced down her spine. "Really?"

Ginger nodded with a knowing grin. "And he never goes out with anyone more than once. He makes sure to never let anyone get too attached to him."

That was interesting. She'd have to see what the night would bring for her. Was this a friendly outing or did he really want to take things to the next level. God, she hoped so.

"Show me what you've got," Ginger said, snapping her out of her daydream.

After going through every outfit in her closet and realizing the clothes in her bag were completely wrong for her date, they came up with the idea of going shopping.

They took Ginger's Jeep and drove into town. They went to one of Leigh's favorite stores before she'd moved away. There were some pretty dresses and two-piece outfits that caught her eye, but Ginger went straight for a burgundy slip dress that reached mid-thigh. "That looks like a nightie."

Ginger waggled her brows. "Good, maybe it'll give him ideas."

She laughed and tried it on. Her red hair popped with the dress and it looked good.

"Come on, let me see!" Ginger yelled.

She sauntered out and did a full twirl. "Well?"

"Oh yeah. You're getting laid, honey." Ginger nodded. "That's the one."

She changed back into her clothes and stopped at the lingerie shop to get something sexier than her plain Jane cotton undies. Afterward, they drove to the Main Street Diner for dinner.

The diner hadn't changed much in the time she'd been gone. "It looks like they did a few renovations."

They slid into a booth and glanced down at the menu.

"They did make a few changes. Fresh paint job. I think they restored the booths," Ginger said glancing around. "Mostly, they have a new chef and everyone's raving over her."

A waitress brought them a pot of coffee, cream and sugar along with two mugs.

"Really?" She filled her mug and stared at Ginger.

Ginger nodded. "Remember Marleen Capple?"

"Of course. We shared a bunch of classes together. We were both in the honor society and business leaders of the future." She added sugar and cream into her coffee, stunned by Ginger's words. "Marleen is the new chef?"

Ginger leaned forward and whispered, "Remember how she moved away one day, and nobody knew what happened?"

Everyone remembered that. It was their senior year when Marleen up and left. There had been a lot of talk that the girl was pregnant and had gone away to have the baby, but she never returned. At least, not while Leigh had been there.

"Did anyone ever find out where she went?"

Ginger shook her head. "One day, she was back, and she became the diner's owner's business partner and new chef. The food is amazing, and she really knows her way around a kitchen."

Leigh glanced toward the cooking area and saw a spiky-haired blonde passing dishes to the wait-staff. Their gazes met and the blonde blinked and frowned. She slipped out of view and Leigh turned back to her coffee.

"So what's good here?" she asked Ginger.

"Everything," Ginger laughed. "Her pot roast is to die for. You really need to try her pancakes, though. I don't know what the hell she puts in them, but you can eat them all day long."

"Leigh? Leigh Hale?"

Leigh glanced to her right and saw the blonde approaching their booth. "Marleen?"

She had to ask because the woman looked so different from what Leigh remembered. Gone were the long blonde curls, replaced with short spiky hair with blue and pink tips. Each arm had a full tattoo sleeve and she had several piercings in her ears and nose.

"That's me." Marleen smiled and Leigh was in shock. It was Marleen.

"Wow," was all Leigh could say and got up to give her old friend a hug.

Marleen laughed and hugged her back. "You look amazing."

Leigh snorted. "You're too kind. I'm surprised to see you here."

Marleen shrugged and Leigh sat down again. "I always felt Denali Ridge was home. It was hard to be gone for so long, but I'm happy to be back." She glanced at Leigh's face. "You're back, too."

Leigh sighed. "Yeah. I'm gonna be here now. Gotta figure out what to do with myself."

"Back at your parents' house?"

"Yeah. Kellan and I share the house now, but he's off traveling the world for his job."

"You look really great," Marleen said again, her smile wide. "I'm so happy to see you.

"Thank you! I'm really excited to try your food."

The waitress came to take their order. Marleen turned to her. "Leave them to me. I know what they want."

Leigh raised her brows and Ginger laughed. "I told you everything is amazing."

"All righty then," Leigh said to Marleen. "Surprise me."

Marleen winked. "You got it."

Surprise them she did. She sent them out pancakes, bacon, pot roast, mashed sweet potatoes, fresh roasted turkey, and enough food to fill their booth table without leaving much space for them to eat.

Ginger gaped at the food and then at Leigh. "I guess we should get to eating, huh?"

Leigh laughed and picked up a pancake and put it on her plate. She might not get to eat everything, but she was sure going to try it all. After dinner, Marleen came back to their table when they were ready to leave.

"Listen," Marleen said. "If you guys aren't too busy, I'd love for you two to come over for pizza and wine."

"Sure," Ginger nodded, agreeing for both of them. "Leigh needs to get out. She's been living in New York too long and needs to make friends again."

Leigh shrugged. "I guess. Sure, we can do pizza and wine."

Like she really needed to be pushed into eating.

Marleen hugged her for long moments again as she readied to walk out. "I'm so happy you're back, Leigh. So happy."

Leigh smiled. "Me, too."

It was nice to catch up with old friends. Though she'd never been very close with Marleen, she'd had so many classes and programs with her that they had no choice but to be friendly. Leigh remembered Marleen's mom and dad as a very serious and religious people. Clearly Marleen had rebelled with the tattoos and piercings because there was no way Mrs. Capple would have approved of Marleen doing any of that. Especially cutting her long curls.

Marleen stood at the door and waved goodbye as they got into Ginger's Jeep.

"I wonder why she left," Ginger asked.

"Me, too."

CHAPTER SEVEN

Leigh took a nice long soak in the tub, shaved her legs and other bits and put lotion on. If she was going to get lucky then so was he. She wanted to be as beautiful and sexy as she could. Friend or not, this was something teenage Leigh had only ever dreamed of. A date with Xander Caze. The thought alone made her stomach quiver.

She tapped her foot on the wood. He wasn't late, she was just nervous. She'd done her makeup carefully. Dressed carefully and chosen her favorite perfume for him. Not that she expected to sleep with Xander, but she wanted him to know she could wear things without stains on them.

The sound of the doorbell made her jump up

on the bed. She knew better than to run down the hall in four-inch heels, so she took her time. When she pulled the door open, she was left speechless.

"Wow," he said, taking the words out of her mouth.

"You...uh...you look pretty wow yourself," she gulped. Wow enough that she would happily raise her dress and sit on his face. Not that he needed to know that.

He offered his hand and she smiled, taking a step toward him when the heel of her shoe caught between two slats of wood. She gasped, ready to fall on her face when he was catching her in his arms, pressing her back against the door to keep her steady.

He was so close. Her heart thudded so loud in her chest, it made it hard to hear herself try to catch her breath.

"You look beautiful, Leigh," he said, his face inches from hers.

"Thank you," she licked her lips and his gaze shot down to her mouth.

Fuck it. A taste never hurt anybody. She was about to find out just how friendly Xander wanted to get. Leaning into his face, she brushed her lips over his. Tingles of electricity rushed through her blood.

His eyes went full on gold and he gave a soft growl. Then he smashed his mouth over hers and left her breathless. The kiss was hungry. Desperate. As if he couldn't get enough of her taste. She moaned, curling her arms around his neck and let him lead her into all the temptation in the world.

Their tongues rubbed and his hand went from holding her arm to gliding down around her hip and cupping her ass. Another growl sounded from him, and she felt her body tingle with need. He was hard. Rock hard. She felt him at the juncture of her thighs.

Her brain cells stopped working when he pressed her into his hardness. Her pussy slickened. Her sex throbbed and her need skyrocketed.

Much to her sadness, he pulled back from their kiss, his teeth nibbling and sucking on her lips. "We can't stay here."

She whimpered. Another kiss. "I know."

"Fuck," he grumbled and swiped his tongue over her mouth. "You taste better than I could have ever imagined."

She wanted to tell him the same thing. This was

so much better than all her fantasies. Nothing beat real life. "Xander."

"Again."

She slid her fingers into his hair and moaned. "Again, what?"

"Say my name like that," he whispered, kissing up her jaw to her ear. "Like you can't wait for me to fuck you all night."

She gulped. "Xander, we should go if we're going to…uh, go."

A soft groan sounded from him. "You're right. Dinner first." He pulled back with a grin. "Dessert later."

Dessert? Was she dessert? Or was he dessert? Yes, he was dessert. She wanted to argue that she liked eating dessert first. Sometimes all she wanted was dessert but didn't want to sound like a desperate nymphomaniac.

He held her hand and helped her into his car. She raised her brows. This was a different car than the one he'd arrived in yesterday afternoon. This one was expensive. Probably limited edition by the brand and the lights. The doors opened upward which was pretty cool.

The night had a slight chill, but she'd grabbed a cute fluffy jacket on her way out. It was one of the few items she'd left at home she still fit into. New York had brought on so much work and stress she'd gained more weight than she cared to admit. She raised her brows at the slow sexy music playing in the car and wondered if those oldies were really his type of music.

"Yes," he chuckled. "I like old school romantic songs. My mother loves them, and I grew up hearing them all the time. I learned to love them."

She smiled and turned in her seat to face him better. "Really? Your mom got you into oldies?"

"My mom can be a very persuasive woman," he said. "She somehow managed to get me and Kellan to take her friend's two daughters to their proms when we were in college." He made a turn and they got on the highway. "Mom said they had few friends and no boys had asked them, but they wanted to go." He flashed his smile at her. "Kellan fell for it first. Then I had to follow."

"Lucky girls. I bet they were the talk of the night with you two as their dates."

He shrugged. "I don't like to brag, but, yeah."

She burst into giggles at his lack of modesty. "How do you even know that?"

"Other girls kept coming up to ask us if we

were really their dates. And if we'd done it for free."

She gasped. "Girls can be so mean." She squeezed his thigh. "That was so nice of you to do. I'm sure they were grateful for that."

"Don't tell anyone, but I get yearly Valentine's Day cards from Janice's husband. He says he's grateful I did that for her that night. It boosted her confidence and when he asked her out the next day she said yes. They've been together ever since."

"Oh, Xander," she sighed. "That's so sweet."

"Did you find what it was you went looking for in New York?" he asked. "I remember Kellan telling me you had decided you needed a change and didn't feel Denali Ridge was the place for you anymore. Is that still the case?"

She glanced out of the windshield, thinking of his question. Leaving had been hard. Coming back had been even harder. "I wanted to make something of myself and I didn't know how I could do that here. I felt like the town was so small and the boardwalk and all those casinos and hotels weren't there back then. There was so little city to speak of. I wanted to experience a big city. The culture. The people." She pressed back in the seat. "I wanted a change."

"How was it?"

She gave a rough laugh. "Not good. New York City will eat people alive if they're not ready for it. It's beautiful and fun for anyone on vacation, but the reality is that you have to be ready to have no life if you're looking to make a career in the financial service industry. I barely slept. I ate poorly and gained crazy weight."

She made a face. "As you can see. But that's not even the worst part. In that massive city with beautiful stores and lights, full of life and emotions, I felt completely alone." She glanced at his driving profile. "I was alone."

"You're here now," he said, grabbing her hand and placing it back on his thigh. "And you're not alone. I'm here with you."

Yes, he was. And he'd kissed her. Oh, mother, how amazing was that kiss that it was still burning on her lips.

They arrived at the boardwalk and parked at one of his hotels. She hadn't been to any of them, but she'd passed by the one he'd opened in New York. It was big and beautiful, and she could barely believe she knew the owner. This one was just as gorgeous. All steel and glass with a unique architecture that reminded her of buildings she'd seen in a co-worker's trip to the United Arab Emirates.

"This is beautiful," she said as they went into the hotel. She was immediately assaulted by the sounds of slots and sirens of people winning at games.

He led her past the casino to the exit by the boardwalk. There they went downstairs to a restaurant at the beach. Part of his hotel, the restaurant had a beautiful pier encased in glass. They sat at the farthest table with no others near them.

The waiter left menus for them and brought a bottle of wine Xander requested. He filled their glasses and left with their orders.

"I can't believe this is all yours," she told him. "Your parents must be so proud. I'm very proud of you."

His gaze scanned her face. "Why?"

"You've made yourself a success. That's not something that happened overnight or even easily. I remember watching you talk to Kellan about how you'd own your own hotel one day." She grinned. "I didn't understand at the time why a hotel was such a big deal. Why didn't you want to own a store?" She laughed. "This is," she motioned to her surroundings, "an empire. Congratulations, Xander."

The vulnerable look in his eyes caught her straight in the chest. He must not get told often what an amazing job he'd done for his family, but he deserved the praise. She was glad he wasn't full of himself, talking nonstop about his money or what he could give her. Getting to know Xander was turning out to be a lot more interesting than she'd realized.

"Thank you. Nobody usually says that to me," he admitted. "My parents expect me to be a leader, so it's no surprise to them that I've made this happen."

She nodded. "I know. But coming from the city where you either make it your bitch or it makes you its bitch, I'm damned proud of your hard work. Your accomplishments should be celebrated," she told him and lifted her glass of wine. "To you."

He shook his head and flashed her a wicked grin. "Not tonight. Tonight is all about us."

Oh. Oh, boy. She was in trouble.

CHAPTER EIGHT

Xander couldn't believe how beautiful she looked. The smile on her face made his heart skip a beat. Her scent of desire for him was making him fucking crazy. All he thought of was kissing her every other second. When she told him she was proud of him, something he hadn't expected happened.

He'd never been concerned with anyone's approval in his life. He'd been raised to be an alpha and knew that the leader of his pride would have to be tough, controlled, aggressive, and demanding. But he'd never been told that he'd seek out his mate's sweet words. He'd never been told that the pride in her eyes over his success would mean more than all the hotels he'd built.

He watched her eat her dinner and loved how she enjoyed her food. She wasn't worried about how much she ate or complained when there was something on her plate she didn't like. She simply moved it off to her bread plate.

"This place is great," she told him, her gaze scanning the restaurant with interest. "I love the setup."

"Thank you. I had an idea and my mother helped make it happen."

Her brows raised. "Your mom?"

"She's a great architect. She helped me bring a lot of visions to life."

"Wow. You come from a family of smart people, huh?" She grinned. "Intelligence is sexy."

"Really? We can go through the proposal for my next project and really make you hot," he joked.

They were having the chocolate souffle for dessert and he loved her reaction to the first bite. She moaned, closing her eyes and almost sighing into her chair.

"This is amazing," she groaned and took another bite. "How can you work here and not eat this all day long?"

He laughed at her shock. "Some nights the hotel chef, who does random overnight hours, will make one and send it to my office. I'm lucky if I get to it before Julian."

"Who's Julian?"

He frowned. "Kellan hasn't mentioned him?"

Her brows puckered and she shook her head slowly. "No. Not really. The name definitely doesn't sound familiar."

"He's my head of security. Second-in-command. A good family friend, too."

"I am surprised you're not married with kids," told him. She kept glancing down at her plate but would take quick peeks every few moments.

"Why are you surprised?"

She jerked her head up and blinked. "Um, because you're you."

What did that mean? "Okay?"

She shook her head. "You're good looking, successful, fun, and," she cleared her throat, "a great kisser."

Her cheeks turned pink giving her an aura of youth he liked. "I hadn't found the right woman. I take marriage seriously. I'm not going to waste mine or anyone's time with half-assed promises that I don't plan to keep. Marriage for me and my people is for life. We don't do divorce."

She nodded slowly and drank her coffee.

"That's impressive. You don't hear men speaking like that nowadays. Most people are lying their way through life."

He saw the hurt in her eyes and hated that someone had done that but was glad it had driven her to him. The fact she was home allowed him the time to spend with her and show her how she belonged with him.

After dinner, they walked down the boardwalk. He held her hand, knowing that he needed that contact with her. It was a strange reality he lived in now. As if all the years of missing her had rushed him, and he and his lion couldn't stand the thought of even a single inch of space between them.

They stopped by the steps that led to the beach and sat on a bench to stare at the moon over the water.

"I'm glad you're back," he said, looking for the right words to express to her how much she meant without scaring her.

"I am, too."

He squeezed her hand in his and brought it to his lips. She watched him kiss her fingers and then the back of her hand. He grabbed a long red curl and tucked it behind her ear, gliding his fingers down her jaw to cup her cheek. "You're so beautiful."

She leaned into his touch and the lion roared for his mate. He needed her. But for now, he'd settle for a kiss. The kiss was soft this time. He let her lead, giving her the freedom to control how far she wanted to go. The tentativeness of her touch almost knocked him to his knees. She was so sweet, her tongue dipping into his mouth and rubbing sensuously against his. Then came the little moans that made him have to fight the lion for control.

His mate was a temptress. She gripped the collar of his suit jacket and moaned louder. He scooped her into his lap, holding her against him and deepening the kiss. The scent of her arousal drove him crazy. He wanted to taste her sweet honey on his tongue and watch her fly apart when she came.

He knew she wanted him, too. And tonight it was her call. He wasn't pushing. Yet. Though his lion wanted him to grab her, take her, and mate her, he'd give her time. Even if it killed him. It just might, too. She moaned into their kiss and wiggled on his lap and he knew he would have a difficult time trying to stay away from her. The sooner he could show her they belonged together, the sooner she'd be his.

He took her home. It was the hardest moment of his life to want to follow her inside but know she had to make that choice. He'd waited for her to say something, but she'd only kissed him goodnight at the door.

He was only a few moments down the road when he glanced at the floor of the passenger seat and noticed she'd dropped her phone. He had to go back and make sure she got it. Not to mention his lion was growling for him to be with her, angry that he'd left her alone to begin with.

CHAPTER NINE

Leigh watched Xander leave from her front door. Damn it. She should've invited him in. She opened her door and frowned. She could've sworn she put the alarm on before she left. She rolled her eyes at herself. Of course. She forgot with her hormones making her stupid. She was surprised she didn't do something worse than that.

Inside the house, she tossed her clutch on a sofa and slipped her jacket off. She turned to go up the hallway to her room when a flash of movement made her glance to the side. She didn't get a chance to do anything. A fist came out of nowhere and slammed to the side of her face. She fell backward, hitting a chair and landing on her back on the carpet.

A scream lodged in her throat. The pain was instant. Tears filled her eyes and fire spread from her lip to her jaw and the side of her face.

She could barely see straight when someone manhandled her onto her feet. "Hello, beautiful," the big beefy man said. He jerked her up and she hit another table, trying to get away from him. "Where are you going, doll? We're just getting started."

"Hey, Niko," another male voice came from behind her. "Let's get her tied up. We have a lot of work ahead of us."

She struggled to get out of the big guy's hold. He had one of her arms, but she scratched his face with her free hand and stomped on his foot with her heel.

"Oh, you're feisty, huh?" he sneered. "I like it when they fight back. Makes it more interesting."

Leigh tried to open her mouth to scream but the taste of blood and shooting pain stopped her. She ended up whimpering and fighting the man's hold until they got by a table with one of the amethyst geodes her mother had always kept on the table. She gripped the side of it and slammed it into his head. He stumbled back, releasing her. She was rushing to the front door when the other guy came out of the kitchen. He ran after her. She jerked the door open then slammed into a body.

She screamed and closed her eyes. When she opened them a millisecond later, she realized it was Xander. He'd come back.

He shoved her behind him and the guy chasing her stopped and pulled out a gun. "Don't get involved."

Xander growled. "Too late."

She watched him rip through his clothes, his body shifting into a massive lion. Her world stopped. Xander Caze was a shifter. How did she not know this? Why did she not know this?

The massive lion roared and dashed toward the guy with the gun. She stared in horror as the guy shot at Xander, but the lion took him down. There was minimal fighting and he had the guy bleeding his guts out on her mother's special rug. The big beefy Niko stumbled into the room rubbing the side of his face. His eyes bugged out when he saw the lion roaring at him, mouth full of blood. His friend's blood.

He jumped back, trying to avoid the animal, but it was no use. The lion hopped over the furniture to get at him. He darted past a sofa and ran toward the kitchen door. They must have gotten in through there because he rushed out without having to turn the lock.

The lion was on his tail and she watched as the big man got to the yard only to be tackled. He yelled, trying to fend off the claws swiping at him. She winced and heard the crunching of bones and the squishy sounds of blood and skin tearing.

Her stomach rolled. She held on to her face while clinging to the door. The guy's head was ripped right off, and she couldn't watch anymore. A wave of dizziness made her slide down until she was sitting at the entrance. Nausea rushed up her throat. She gagged and noticed her leg was bleeding. Then she glanced at her hand and noticed it was bleeding, too.

Her dress was torn, and she had bruises on her legs. She was trying to make sense of what happened when Xander's naked body bent down and scooped her up. He carried her to his car.

She groaned in pain.

"It's going to be okay, Leigh," he told her, his voice gruff with apparent emotion. "I'm taking you to a hospital. They'll take care of you. I'm not going to leave you alone."

"How did you know to come back?" She winced and spoke softly, not wanting to move her jaw.

"You dropped your phone and I figured I'd come back then I heard you scream. You opened the door at the moment I was going to break it down." He caressed her hand, his face full of worry. "You're going to be okay."

She nodded and closed her eyes. The ringing in her ears continued but the nausea slowed until blackness took over.

CHAPTER TEN

Leigh woke in a hospital bed. The pain in her jaw had diminished but she felt her face was swollen.

"You're awake," Xander said from beside her. "How do you feel?"

"Less pain," she mumbled. "Face is swollen. I look bad, right?"

"You're beautiful. Swollen or not."

A doctor came into the room and looked at her. "Oh, good. You're awake. Okay, Leigh. I'm Dr. Burnside."

"Where am I?"

Dr. Burnside cleared his throat. "This is a private medical facility for area shifters."

She blinked. That's right. Last night, she'd seen

Xander shift into a lion. A huge lion with a golden mane and massive teeth. She'd also seen him kill two men for her. To save her.

"The good news," Dr. Burnside started, "is that nothing is broken. Your jaw took a hit but luckily all you have is swelling. We gave you some medication for pain to help you while the swelling reduces."

"Thank you," she said. "I can go home then?"

He nodded. "I'll give you some meds to take with you and just come back if you experience any more nausea or vomiting. We did a scan, and all looks good, but if you feel strange, don't hesitate to come back." He turned to Xander. "Make sure she's not alone for the next forty-eight hours. Just a precaution."

"She won't be. I'm taking her home with me."

Home. She waited until the doctor left before she turned to Xander. "My house is a mess, isn't it?"

"Your house is going to be fine. I've sent Julian to get it cleaned up. The sheriff is sending someone to dispose of the bodies." He squeezed her hand. "Did they tell you what they wanted?"

"No. They just attacked the moment I was by the hall. I think I walked in on something."

"Like a robbery?"

She winced. "Maybe. They said they were going to tie me up so they could get to work, so I guess I interrupted them."

"Hmm."

A few hours later, they were at Xander's house. She had never even thought of the fact he had his own place. She figured since he owned so many hotels that he might just live in one of them.

They went up a long dirt drive off the main road and then reached a gated entrance. There, the gate opened, and the road turned paved. It was beautiful. The trees hung over each other in a beautiful arch toward the house. The cabin in the woods took her breath away.

Massive logs created a two-story structure with lots of glass windows to look out. There was a big wraparound porch with rocking chairs and even a lower level, since the cabin was built on a slant.

"This is your house?"

"Yeah," he said and went around the other side to help her out of the car. She got out feeling like an old person who'd just been through the boxing ring. "Here, let me help you."

She allowed him to carry her up the steps to the porch. There he put her down and she gaped at the beauty of it all. The sound of water rushing made her take steps to one side to see a stream of water that seemed to grow as it went farther from the house.

"You have a lake?"

He chuckled at her surprise. "Yeah. Most of the mountain homes around here have access to some kind of stream that leads to the Denali Ridge River. My parents have front door access to it."

"You definitely do not see this in the city." She walked back to him and went inside his home. It was rustic and perfect. Minimal and clean. She loved it. "You live here by yourself?"

"Yes. I am not the type to be under my parents' thumb. When I returned from working overseas, I set about building the cabin and their business along with my own."

"This is amazing. I can't even imagine living in all this every day," she gushed. He grabbed her hand and led her to the kitchen. "This is paradise. Surely."

"Maybe you can consider living in paradise?" he asked and led her to a dining room table where she sat and glanced at his kitchen. It was massive with professional appliances that would make any chef jealous. Hell, she wasn't a cook and was getting the urge to make something just to use the beautiful space.

Consider living in paradise? As in Denali Ridge? She really had no choice at the moment. New York seemed like a lifetime away. Her regrets over leaving to begin with were weighing on her. She wanted to just do something right for once. Going into the concrete jungle had done nothing but bring stress and sadness into her life. Just being back in her hometown had calmed most of her fears and given her a sense of hope.

But what would she do about a job? She could figure it out. Take some classes. Learn something new. She might not have most of her savings, but she had some assets she could still use. Her trust from her parents' estate. If anything she could sell her half of the house to Kellan and use the money to start fresh.

"You're thinking really hard," he said.

She jerked a glance at his direction. He was busy brewing coffee in a very cool espresso machine.

"I'm sorry. I'm thinking of ways to restart my life. New York isn't going to happen again. I'm not interested in going back." She lifted her arms and then let them drop slowly. "I realize that it's not for me. Being here has always felt like home. I tested the waters because I wanted to see what was out there for me."

He nodded and placed the two cups on saucers and carried them to the table where she sat. He placed one in front of her. "It's a latte. You ordered one after dinner. You like it, right?"

There he went paying attention to her likes like she was so interesting, and he needed to know everything about her. She blinked up at him. "I do. Thanks."

"So what did you find testing the waters?"

She snorted and picked up her cup. "That I should've stayed my ass here. Now, I don't even want to go back into banking."

"What else interests you?"

"I minored in accounting so I can always find something doing that." She rubbed her forehead. "I'm getting a headache just thinking about this."

"Leave it," he said. "I have something I have to do in a couple of days and I'm hoping you want to join me."

"What's that?"

"You'll see. I promise it'll be fun."

She grinned, drained the rest of her cup, and sighed. "I'm suddenly exhausted."

He stood and took her hand. "Come on. I'll show you to your room."

She really wanted to stay with him. In his room. But she looked a sight and the pain was real. They went up the stairs. Biting down on her tongue to stop herself from groaning at the pain, she let out a slow breath with each step. They were midway up the stairs when he lifted her into his arms and carried her the rest of the way.

"Don't argue with me, Leigh," he said, his golden gaze on hers. "You don't need to be brave for me. I'm here to help you however necessary."

Her eyes filled with tears. Fuck, she was turning into such a sap, but nobody other than Kellan ever said things like that to her. Her only experience with a man being kind were all tied to her brother. Even her father had been of the mindset that she needed to be strong, so he wasn't someone she could go to for cuddling or even a hug.

"Thank you," she mumbled, fighting back the urge to cry.

He took her into a beautiful bedroom in cream and yellow. The theme of the room looked like old Victorian.

"This is beautiful."

He grinned. "Glad you like it. I'll be sure to let my mother know that her girly room is Leigh approved."

She smiled and kissed his cheek. He stared at her as if surprised by her actions. She was damned surprised herself that she'd done that, but she hadn't realized how kind he was. This version of Xander was new and someone she really liked.

He left her on the bed and pointed to a closet. "There's clothes in there. I got you some things." His face turned a bright red and she frowned. "I picked everything myself, so I hope I got your tastes and sizes right."

The thoughtfulness of his actions made her heart squeeze. He'd gone out and bought her clothes and things she would need to stay with him.

"Thank you."

"There's some other stuff in the drawers, too," he added, and met her gaze. "Call me if you need me."

She gave a slight nod and watched him walk out. Her heart was tripping over itself and her breaths were coming out in a rush. She opened the drawers and saw underwear from her favorite store in her size. She also saw brand new pajamas.

There were clothes in the closet. Stuff that was very much her style and that would fit her.

He didn't have to buy her clothes, he could've just brought stuff from her home, but the fact he had showed her how much thought he put into her being in his home.

The next morning she woke to the scent of coffee. Xander was standing next to her bed wearing a dark pair of jeans that clung to his hips like they'd been made for him. He also wore an old school T-shirt that had a Coca-Cola bottle on it.

She raised her brows and shook her head. "Coke? Really? I thought you had better taste than that."

He chuckled and offered her coffee. "I know you're a lemonade girl, but when it comes to soda, Coke is the best."

She rolled her eyes. "Pepsi. All day, every day." Then she put cream and sugar in her coffee and took a sip. "Thank you so much."

He sat beside her on the bed. "I recall how you get without coffee and wanted to make sure you weren't going to throw anything at me for waking you without your caffeine."

She made a face but then laughed at the truth in his words. "Yeah, okay. You're right."

"How do you feel?"

She touched her face. "Better." And winced at how tender it felt. "Is it really bad?"

He shook his head. "We can tell people you got into a fight with a bear."

She choked on her coffee and sputtered a laugh. "A bear? That bad?"

"No, but if we say a bear, they're going to say you must've done great because you don't look bad enough to have gotten into a fight with a bear."

She giggled at his words. "I like how you think. A bear fight it is then."

"I hope you don't mind if we have some company later."

She raised her brows. "What do you mean?"

"I've allowed some of the local elementary school kids to come over later for an outdoor movie outing. Not during school hours for this one. This will be for their extended after school for parents who work late, and their kids have to stay longer."

"Really? How's that gonna work?"

"I host it every few months for them," he told her. "The teachers sometimes run out of ideas on how to get them out without spending money or having the parents pay for expensive trips. Usually by four or five I've set up an outdoor screen and everyone brings a blanket. They grab a cushion from a pile I keep, and they watch the movie on a projector I set up."

"Xander, that's really sweet."

He shrugged. "One of my employees had told me that her son's teacher was always trying to come up with cheap outing ideas for the kids and that one came to me. I also let them come on the property and do picnics by the stream. They do birdwatching and study different plants, too."

"Wow. You are amazing."

"Nah. I just like being able to help out the teachers and parents that need it."

Her heart melted over his kindness and how unfazed he was by how giving that was of him.

After she'd showered and changed, the children arrived and were already set up when she went downstairs. The back yard was full of blankets and pillows and the kids sat on them in sets of two.

"Hi," she said joining Xander and two other women by the projector.

"You should've waited for me to come up and get you," he said. "I know how your body hurt going up those stairs."

She blushed, aware that the two women were watching and listening.

"It's okay. I do feel better today," she turned to the women. "Hi, I'm Leigh."

"Vella and Dina," Xander said, "Leigh is a family friend."

The women smiled and shook her hand. She wanted him to say she was his girlfriend and that thought made her pause. Why did it matter? Neither of the women were flirting with him. But she realized that she had started thinking more and more of something deeper going on between them.

"What are we watching?" she asked.

"Xander's great," Vella said. "He got them a Disney movie and we get a break to grade some work while they enjoy their outing and the snacks he set up for them."

Leigh glanced at the table with food and drinks. "You're a great host, aren't you?"

Dina snorted. "I wish he'd host something like this for the teachers, too." She laughed and elbowed Vella. "We like snacks and movies, too."

Everyone laughed and the teachers went to sit with two students. Leigh stayed next to Xander, watching him set the projector. He took her hand and they sat on a blanket under a tree.

"I hate this movie," she whispered into his ear.

"What?" He gasped. "How can you not like *The Lion King*?"

She sniffled when the father lion got killed and the baby lion's horrified reality took over the screen. "That's why. I hate that part. The father dies. I know it's just a small part of the movie," she cuddled into his side, "but it's still really sad."

"It is a sad part," he said and rubbed her arm, hugging her tightly.

A little girl in front of them turned around and patted Leigh's foot. "It's okay. My mom said we don't need to cry because it's just a movie and the papa lion isn't really dead," she said with a serious face. "He is acting. That means he is faking it. When they finished filming, he was alive and went home with his baby lion."

Leigh gave the little girl a smile. "Thank you. That makes me feel so much better."

The little girl nodded and turned back to the movie.

CHAPTER ELEVEN

Xander had Julian looking into what happened at Leigh's house. The fact two males broke in and hurt her had made his lion so angry, he didn't want to be more than two feet away from her. But not knowing why they'd broken into her house was an even bigger issue. If it was a robbery, then she'd walked in at the wrong time. But what if it wasn't? What if it was her ex or even someone coming after Kellan from his job?

He couldn't stand the idea of Leigh being hurt again. So he was going to make sure she wasn't left alone again.

He watched her interact with a couple of the children. Her conversation with them was animated and interesting. The image of her with their children filled his chest with emotion. He needed to figure out a way to show her they were meant to be together.

After the children left, she helped him clean up the yard and then they went inside. The knock at the front door was one he'd been expecting.

"Come on," he said. "There's some people I want you to meet."

She raised her brows and went to the front door with him.

"Mom," he said, pulling his mother into his arms and hugging her. "This is Leigh." He glanced at Leigh. "This is my mom, Belinda."

Leigh's eyes widened and she smiled at his mom. He sensed her concern and noticed her shifting from foot to foot. "It's nice to meet you."

"Oh, honey," his mom said and pulled Leigh into her arms. "We don't shake hands in this family. We hug."

Leigh laughed and hugged her back. "Thank you."

"And this is Julian," he said to Leigh. "He's my security chief and a good friend."

Julian grinned and shook her hand. "At the risk

of getting myself killed, I'll stick to shaking your hand."

"Nice to meet you, Julian."

"Come on in, you two. I've been waiting for you."

His mom gave him a look. "Don't start. I had a lot of cooking to do. Julian, get the food from the car. Leigh and I are going to the kitchen and have some coffee."

Leigh blinked. "Oh, okay."

He watched them head to the kitchen and turned to Julian. "Let's get the food. Any news on the two guys?"

"No. They had zero ID on them and I'm pretty sure they weren't locals. Nobody has reported anyone missing around here."

"Great. What about her ex? Anything there?" He opened the trunk of Julian's SUV and was taken aback by the amount of metal trays. "Are we hosting some type of party I'm not aware of?"

Julian shrugged. "You know your mother better than anyone. When has she ever cooked small amounts?"

True. His mother loved caring for and feeding everyone. It's one of the reasons she'd made such a great leader alongside his father. Now it was

Xander who led, and he wondered how Leigh would feel about being an alpha's mate. Would she hate the idea? Would she reject him over that role?

"I found nothing bad or illegal on the ex-boyfriend. He's got a financial services company, but everything is legal, and his reviews are great. He offers a decent return on investments for his customers. Better than most banks."

Xander frowned. He knew enough about investments that it was a red flag. For anyone to offer a higher return on investment than normal meant they were doing something that would eventually catch up to them.

"So his company is stable?"

Julian nodded and picked up one pile of trays while Xander grabbed the rest.

"Everything that I've been told so far is on the up and up."

"Dig deeper. There's something there. For her to run the way she did, he did something to scare her."

They found his mom and his mate in the kitchen making lemonade.

"After all the times he's seen me make lemonade from scratch," his mother told Leigh with disgust, "he makes it with this powdered crap."

Leigh grinned and gave him a guilty look. "I use that at home, too."

"Oh, no," his mom groaned. "I will teach you the best way to make homemade lemonade," she said happily.

"Not unless you want me to poison someone," Leigh laughed. "I suck at anything food related. Powdered lemonade is one of the few things I've mastered." She met Xander's gaze. "That and ordering pizza."

"Tomasino's?" his mom asked.

"Yeah," Leigh cleared her throat.

"I get that. They are pretty freaking good."

His mom spread the trays over his kitchen island and created a buffet. She opened up all the aluminum trays and shoved serving spoons into each.

"This is a lot of food," Leigh said. "But it all looks amazing."

His mother beamed and handed her a plate. "I hope you like it. Go on and serve yourself. You're our guest of honor."

Leigh glanced at Xander but went ahead and

served herself pasta, chicken, salad, and a dinner roll.

The rest of them filled plates with food and sat at the kitchen table where the lemonade, glasses, and silverware were already set up.

"You know, Leigh," his mom started, "Kellan slept at my house more than he did at yours."

Leigh nodded. "I remember. I always wanted to go with him, but he was adamant that it was his time with his friend, and I wouldn't have any fun over there."

His mom gave Xander a look. "Oh, I don't know. I'm sure I could've taught you how to cook while the boys were tossing themselves off the house onto the trampoline."

Leigh's eyes popped wide. "They what?"

His mom nodded. "Off the house to the trampoline. They also did it into the pool, too." She sighed. "I had a hell of a time making sure nobody broke any bones." She smacked Xander's arm. "This one would heal quickly, but poor Kellan would've been stuck with a cast for god knows how long."

"That's right," Leigh said, meeting his gaze. "Shifters heal fast, don't you?"

"Yes," Xander replied.

"Why didn't I know you were a shifter? I just found out when I saw you turn into a massive lion in my living room. I thought that guy hit me hard enough that I was seeing things."

He heard the hurt in her voice. She felt like he'd kept a part of himself from her. "I'm sorry, Leigh. I don't know. I guess Kellan never told you. He and your parents always knew."

"They did?" she gasped, her tone even more confused than before.

He couldn't explain it either. He didn't know she wasn't aware. Her family had chosen not to tell her. "I guess maybe because we had such little interaction, they didn't feel the need to have to tell you and possibly scare you?"

She gave him a look as if he'd lost his mind. "Scare me? I would've never been scared of you."

The lion inside him wanted to roar and the look she gave him made him love her even more.

CHAPTER TWELVE

After dinner, they started playing Monopoly and Leigh found out just how competitive Xander truly was. She'd been lucky in her turns and had bought property and set about putting hotels and houses to collect rent.

"You owe me," she laughed when he landed on one of her properties. "And they call you a hotel king."

He handed her the cash with a serious face. "You could've held out for better property."

She nodded. "Yeah, I could have. But I like these." She fanned her face with the money he handed her. "And I like getting paid."

Belinda laughed and watched them bicker over

who owed who rent and whose property was better.

"Looks like she's just as competitive as you are, Xander."

Leigh didn't realize she'd been egging him on but laughed at the look of surprise he gave her. "I can be pretty cutthroat."

He raised his brows. "Put your money where your mouth is."

"Oh? What do you have in mind?"

"Whoever ends the game with the most money wins."

She glanced at her stack of cash and nodded. "Okay and what exactly do I win?"

"Whatever you want."

Oh. Oh, wow. That was a dangerous offer.

She gave him a curious look. "What do you get if you win?"

His eyes flashed gold. "Whatever I want."

Yeah. It was definitely a dangerous game.

"Sounds like I should start thinking of what I want," she taunted.

He chuckled and rolled his dice.

An hour later, both Belinda and Julian had given up their properties in bankruptcy but neither wanted to leave. They watched them both try to one up each other.

"Come on," Belinda said to Leigh. "You've got this. He can't compete with all those hotels. Take him down!"

"Mom!" he hollered.

"What?" Belinda grinned. "Girls gotta stick together."

"Forget that," Julian said and slapped him on the shoulder. "You can take her. You've got the strongest row and enough hotels on there to break her with one bad roll of the dice."

She gulped. It was time to roll. She tossed the dice and secretly wished she'd lose. Not that she wanted to. But curiosity had her wondering what he'd ask for. Of course, her dignity told her to get her shit together and win this bitch. Kellan was as competitive as they came. He'd raised her to be just like him when it came to board games.

"Give it up, princess," he said, a dangerous grin on his face. "You landed on one of my most expensive properties."

She paid up and he rolled. Damn it. He landed on his own property. Another roll and she paid him again. It went south from there for her. Soon she was selling and mortgaging everything, until the clock hit ten and they called the end of the game.

She counted her money and he counted his.

"You can still win," Belinda said reassuringly. She was so cute.

"No, she can't," Julian chuckled. "You know she lost big time."

At the count of their money, she lost by ten dollars. Julian and Belinda left after that. The moment she closed the door behind them and turned around, Xander was there, pressing her into the wood and meeting her gaze.

"Time to pay up."

CHAPTER THIRTEEN

Leigh curled her arms around his neck and rose to her tip toes to press their lips together. The first swipe of his tongue over hers felt decadent. Her lungs felt tight and her breaths came in short spurts. The kiss was deep and hungry, and she groaned, pressing herself into him.

A soft growl sounded from him and he picked her up and set her in front of the dining room table where they'd been eating. He tugged her shorts down along with her underwear and then her T-shirt came off. She stood bare in front of him.

This should have been the time to be filled with embarrassment or something, but all she wanted was more of his touch. The way he looked at her made feel strong and beautiful. He cupped her breasts and she sucked in a breath, pressing her chest into his hands.

"So beautiful," he growled. "So soft."

She moaned and pulled him down for another kiss. He lifted her onto the table, spreading her thighs and caressing her pussy with a hand. "You're so hot, Leigh," he groaned between kisses. "Slick."

She kissed his neck and groaned at how good he smelled. In the past, she hadn't been so aware of a male's scent as she was now. She nibbled on his neck and he growled softly. Before she got a chance to keep kissing him, he pulled a chair and sat, his face level with her sex. She leaned back on her elbows and watched him place her thighs on his shoulders. A gasp was all that escaped her when he slid his tongue into her pussy.

"Xander!" she called out and caught herself. Biting her lip, she gripped the edges of the table and held on. He pressed his whole face into her, rubbing himself into her folds as if he wanted her wetness all over himself. He ate her pussy like she was his lunch. As if all the food he'd just had meant nothing because this was what he truly wanted.

Her. She wiggled her hips and let out a soft whimper.

Another lick and she was shaking, trying not to fall back and hit her head on the table. He pinched one of her nipples with a hand, tugging and tweaking, making her rock harder into his face.

"Xander, God. Please," she gasped.

His face was all in her sex, his tongue deep in her channel. She moaned and rocked, feeling his beard rub along her sensitive folds. She ached hard, her pussy clamped around his tongue, but it wasn't enough. She needed him deep inside her, taking her, loving her, and branding her. She had never wanted a man the way she did him.

"Don't stop," she mumbled.

He groaned into her pussy and she let go. Her body tensed and then a shockwave of pleasure spread through her. She sucked in a breath and let it out slowly. Xander was still licking her inner thigh, biting and growling into her flesh.

She was still shaking and gasping for air when he carried her to her bed. Placing her at the center of the mattress, he shrugged out of his clothes and she welcomed him with open thighs. He caged her with his body, the head of his cock pressing at her entrance and his gaze on her face.

"I can't promise this will be soft and sweet," he growled, his voice rough. "But I can promise you're going to come again, love."

She locked her knees behind his hips and pushed him into her with the balls of her feet. They both groaned as he pressed into her, stretching and filling her with his hardness.

"So good, Xander," she moaned.

He pulled back and thrust deep, making her whimper. There was no slow. He'd told her that. He drove deep and pulled back, his cock burning her with how hot he felt inside her. With every thrust and retreat, she choked, trying to catch her breath. Every time she thought he'd slow down, he went faster. Harder. Deeper.

His body was sliding and gliding over hers as they were both coated in sweat. In. Out. Deep. Rough.

"Fuck," he grunted and drove deep.

She licked her dry lips and moaned again. There was nothing for her to do but widen her legs and let him own her. She loved the feel of him inside her. The way he squeezed her hips, scratching her with how hard her held her.

Another growl sounded from him and she whimpered at the way her pussy fluttered around his cock. She was so close. Her body tensed and then he thrust hard enough to make her scream.

Her body shuddered. Her orgasm tore through her like a tsunami. She clawed at his shoulders, clinging to him and calling for him. He thrust once. Twice. And tensed, his cock seeming to grow inside her. Then he was pulsing and filling her with his cum.

A loud groan sounded from him as he jerked into her. They both panted, breathless and overheated. He held her, keeping himself inside her and flipped them over for her to lie on top of him, her legs to either side of his hips.

"God, Leigh," he murmured, kissing her sweaty forehead and pushing her hair away from her face. "You're perfect, love. Absolutely, perfect."

She gulped and sighed. "We can debate who the real perfect one here is, but I think I'm too relaxed to argue." She kissed his neck and closed her eyes. "Thank you."

"For what, love?"

"Being you."

CHAPTER FOURTEEN

In her bedroom at Xander's home, Leigh glanced at her face and was happy to notice the swelling was completely gone and all that was left was slight yellow bruising. She dressed up for her outing with Xander in a maxi dress and a pair of sandals. The day was warm so she was glad she could wear something lightweight. Still, she grabbed a jacket and went downstairs to wait for him.

He'd gone to one of the hotels for a bit to handle a problem. Wandering the home, she opened up a door she hadn't noticed before and found his home office. The space was absolutely masculine. All dark cherry wood and the scent of her man made her girl parts come to life.

Calm the fuck down, Leigh. He's not even home. She laughed at herself and went over to his bookshelf. She scanned everything and was caught off guard when she saw photo albums.

She pulled one out and sat to look through it. It was photos of Xander as a little kid. He was playing in most of them. There were a bunch of pictures of him with Kellan and she laughed remembering how crazy they'd been back then.

Speaking of her brother, she pulled her cell phone out and dialed his number. She knew Xander had been speaking to him, but she needed to let him know she was okay in her own words.

"Leigh?" He sounded like he'd just woken up. "Is everything okay? Are you okay? Where's Xander?"

"Everything's okay," she told him. "I just wanted to make sure you knew I'm doing good."

"Xander's taking care of you?"

She grinned. "He is. Don't worry. I'm okay." She bit her lip. "I haven't gone back to the house." She sighed. "Not that I'm scared, but I've just been staying with him while my face heals."

Kellan cursed. "I can't believe I wasn't there to help you. I'm so sorry."

"Hey," she said, "I'm not calling to make you feel

bad. I wanted to make sure you knew things are okay and under control so no need to worry."

"Any news from that detective in New York?"

She frowned. "No. I'm going to give him a call. He did say that these types of investigations take time."

"Has your ex tried to contact you?"

She didn't lie to Kellan. Ever. "Yes. He's called many times, but the phone has been on silent, so I don't hear it. He left several messages saying he wants to figure things out."

"You're not really considering it, are you?" he asked with alarm.

"Of course not," she exclaimed. "That would be one of the dumbest moves of my life. Besides," she cleared her throat, "there seems to be something going on with me and Xander. I have to see where this goes."

"Are you sure you want to go there?"

She frowned. "He's your best friend. You have reservations about him or me?"

"Neither. I'm just not sure that you understand how shifters work."

She continued glancing through the photos. "How do they work?"

"Leigh, you can't just break up with Xander when you get tired or bored."

"I don't break up with people because I get tired or bored."

Kellan barked a laugh. "Yes. You do. Every single time. That's why I'm telling you what I'm telling you. Shifters are not like regular human males." He sighed. "Xander's a great guy, but he is possessive, aggressive, and if he feels you're the one he wants, there's no breaks, time apart, or divorce if you ever get married. There's only forever. So you really need to think about this before you get involved with him." He exhaled loudly. "I don't want to see either one of you hurt. I love you both."

She stopped when she found a Polaroid photo of her and Xander the day she'd pretended to marry him. She saw the look of adoration in her eyes and the sweet smile on his face. God. How could she think she was ever going to outgrow her feelings for him? All these years had only made her feel more, deeper.

"I understand," she said. "You don't need to worry. I won't make any decision lightly. I don't want to hurt him either. He's a great man and deserves to be with someone who's going to be there how he needs."

"You deserve the same," Kellan told her. "Just make sure when you are making these decisions, they're based out of love and not fear. Fear makes it hard for us to take chances on what we want in life."

How was she supposed to do that? All her decisions had been terrible so far. She'd moved and made her own life harder. Every man she'd ever dated before Xander had made her realize she was unhappy with him to the point she'd always broken things off.

She wanted Xander. So badly. She wanted to keep him and start a long-lasting relationship with him, but she also didn't want to make any more bad decisions. She was tired of wasting her time. She didn't want to waste Xander's time, either.

The Polaroid of them was such a beautiful moment in their history. She pulled it out of the album and slipped it in her pocket.

"Thanks, Kellan," she said softly. "I just don't know what's right for me anymore." She shook her head. "I don't know what path I'm supposed to take. I'm unsure where to go from here."

"Think back to when you knew what you

wanted out of life," he said. "Take yourself back there. What drives you? What do you want to do with yourself?"

"I'll have to think about that," she told him. "Okay, you get some sleep. I love you."

"I love you, too, sis."

She hung up and sat there thinking of what Kellan had said to her. Her entire childhood had been filled with a ton of activities. Her parents had told her to try everything and see what called to her. She'd wanted to be like them, to please them, so she'd gone into banking. But thinking back, she'd never truly enjoyed that.

Her thoughts went to her years of painting. Though she'd only done it as a hobby, that's what had made her feel grounded. Happy. Her time in New York had only been bearable because she'd set up an easel and oil paints by a window. When she got up every morning, she took an hour to paint while drinking her coffee. Then she'd get ready for work and do the same at night before bed.

Painting. She should try that again. She hadn't done it in weeks and that was one way she found she enjoyed relaxing.

When Xander picked her up, she was deep in

thought. He scared the crap out of her when he walked into his office.

"Are you okay?" he asked, his voice full of concern.

She nodded and jumped to her feet, rushing over to throw herself in his arms. Never in her life had a man made her feel so cherished with something as simple as a hug.

"I'm good. Just thinking."

He kissed her slow and sweet, their lips rubbing on each other and his hands gliding up and down her back to squeeze her ass. Groaning and pulling back, he met her gaze and licked his lips. "We should go."

They got into his SUV and headed into town. She glanced at his profile and felt her heart fill with all kinds of emotions for him. How was this supposed to work? She didn't trust her feelings this quickly after she'd made the shitty decision of being with William. Not that she'd ever felt anything anywhere near this for him, but she was prone to making shitty choices.

She glanced around at the local roller-skating rink. The parking lot was packed. They got out of the car and saw a bunch of kids going in.

"I think we're intruding into someone's private

event," she said at the entrance. The rink was full of boys and girls, all dressed in cute seventies gear.

"Nope." He winked and led her to the skate registration.

"Xander!" A teenage girl with braces grinned and greeted him. "You made it." Her eyes focused on Leigh and her smile widened even more. "And you brought a date."

"Okay," Leigh whispered, "what's going on?"

The teenager giggled. "As you can see, tonight is the middle school's skate night. Xander is the sponsor and also one of the chaperones."

Leigh's gaze jerked to Xander. "You? A chaperone?"

He shrugged. "What can I say? My mom volunteered me, and I couldn't say no."

The girl handed Leigh a pair of new socks and house skates in her size. Xander had his own pair of skates he kept in the place. He guided her to the rink, and she grabbed him for dear life. "Xander, I, uh, haven't done this before."

He chuckled and pulled her slowly. "You mean in all those activities your mother had you do when you were a kid, skating wasn't included?"

She narrowed her eyes. "Ha-ha. No, it wasn't.

I'm not very coordinated," she admitted. "We found out the hard way."

He laughed again and pulled her around the rink. She felt ridiculous to be the only adult struggling to skate when there were eight-year-olds doing figure eights like they were going to the Olympics.

"How the hell are they doing that?" she grumbled.

"Kids are naturally better balanced than adults," he told her.

"Yeah, right," she snorted. "I wasn't."

"That's because you're much better at other stuff," he told her and let go of one hand to pull her along next to him.

"Yeah?" she asked, her heart beating double time in her chest. "Like what?"

"You're funny and you're very clean and organized."

She thought back to the mess in her closet and groaned. "No, I'm not. Try again."

His lips twitched but he didn't laugh at her. "You're determined. You're good with kids. You're sweet and kind. I know you have hidden talents you're not thinking about."

She had been so busy listening to him that she

didn't realize she'd started skating a lot more smoothly than the choppy skate-walking she'd been doing.

"That's really nice of you to say. I'm going to have to figure out what to do with myself soon."

He pulled her into his arms and lifted her off the ground while he continued to skate. "There's no rush to make a decision that could impact the rest of your life, Leigh. It's okay to think about what you want to do and how to pursue your next set of goals."

She stared deep into his eyes and leaned in to kiss him. He was right. She needed to cut herself some slack. In the meantime, she could enjoy their budding relationship. After all, she loved spending time with Xander. He made her feel loved. And as scary as that was, it was a feeling she was enjoying more and more each passing day.

CHAPTER FIFTEEN

Leigh slipped out of Xander's SUV and glanced at her house. There were two bouquets of flowers at her door. Both massive. She glanced over her shoulder at him as she marched up the steps. His brows were drawn down and his lips pressed into a tight line.

She picked up one of the arrangements and opened the front door. A sliver of fear coursed through her at the thought of someone being in there, waiting for her. But she was shocked to find that everything was clean and back in place.

Placing the bouquet on her dining room table, she walked around the house, looking for signs of broken furniture and glanced down at what she remembered to be bloodied carpeting. It looked brand new.

"You did this?" She turned to him. He placed the second bouquet of flowers next to the first and marched up to her.

She slipped her arms around his neck. "Thank you. I don't know what to say."

"I didn't want you to come back and find this place a mess. You know I had Julian handle the cleanup. He was happy to." He kissed her forehead and squeezed her tightly. "Are you sure you want to be here? You can stay with me."

She grinned and nodded. "I know, but I need some time to think. I have to figure out what I'm doing." She kissed his chin. "I love being at your place, but I came here to figure myself out, not to become your problem."

"You're not a problem," he said gruffly. "I love having you with me."

"I just need some time."

He sighed. "I understand. But I'm having some of my men around your area to make sure you're safe."

She laughed. "If that makes you feel better."

"What would make me feel better is to have you

under my roof, but since you're not making it easier, this will have to do."

"Thank you," she said and glanced around. "I'll keep the alarm on at all times."

"If you change your mind, just come over to my place or drive over to the hotel," he said, and she walked him back to the front door. "If anything feels off, call me right away."

"I will," she kissed his lips and leaned on the door, watching him shuffle to his SUV. He sat in his vehicle while she locked the door and turned the alarm on.

Once he was gone, she rushed over to the flowers and opened the cards.

Leigh

I've missed you

XO

She gulped. William. He signed all his gifts with XO. Her stomach churned and nausea rolled up the back of her throat. Fuck. She was afraid to look at the second arrangement but did anyway.

I'll see you soon.

Love

Kellan

Her heartbeats slowed down. Thank god that one was from her brother. The idea that William had sent flowers to her house in Denali Ridge made her feel sick. He knew where she was.

Fear made her chest tighten and her breathing turn shallow. Should she go back to Xander's place? She didn't want to ignore the decisions she had to make because she was so wrapped up in him. She really had to figure out what she was going to do about a job.

Her cell phone rang while she put her clothes away after doing the laundry.

"Hi, Ginger."

"I heard about the break-in," Ginger said. "I'm so sorry. Are you okay?"

"Yeah. I didn't mean to ignore your calls," she said, "but I was pretty out of it for a few days."

"I understand. I was wondering if you wanted some company for dinner?"

She winced. "I hadn't even thought that far ahead. Xander's handling some business with his security chief at the office, so I don't really know what I'm doing."

"Marleen called and suggested we bring the food to you. So you can have a girls' night in. How does that sound to you?"

"That doesn't sound bad, actually. If you guys want to come over, that'd be okay with me."

"Cool. Marleen is bringing the food and I've got dessert. See you soon."

She took a shower and got dressed. Her phone rang again. This time it was Xander.

"Hey," she said, grinning at the fact he'd called her. Seeing his name on the screen gave her butterflies.

"Hi, love. How's everything been so far?"

She lay on her bed and stared at the ceiling. "Good. Honestly, I'd been a little worried about being here again, but I refuse to be pushed out of my house. Not because of fear."

"Nothing has happened, right?"

"Nope. All is good. Ginger and Marleen are coming over in a little while."

"Marleen? Marleen Capple?"

"Yeah, you know her?"

"She co-owns the diner," he said. "I had no idea you knew her."

"We went to school together. Had all the same classes. She was in almost every program and sporting event I was a part of. Her mom must have really wanted to keep her busy, too."

"She's only been back about six months," he said.

"Do you know why she left?" she asked, her

curiosity getting the best of her.

"I thought she'd had a problem with her parents, and they sent her to live at a group home or something. That's what my mother said at the time."

Marleen? Teenage Marleen had been anything but a rebel. She'd been so strict and by the book, she made Leigh feel like a slouch most of the time.

"Anyway, they're coming over for girls' night. So don't worry about me."

"I would be there if it weren't for some trouble we're having with some out of town shifters at the casino. I'll be there for a bit."

"It's okay," she told him. She knew he had businesses to run and she wasn't going to stop him from doing his job just because she was lonely. That was the biggest reason why she needed to find something to do with herself.

"My friend Ryan and his wife Parker are hosting a couples' night tomorrow and wanted to know if we'd like join them."

"Couples' night? What's that?"

"We do some activity and possibly play games and have dinner. This is the first one I've been invited to."

She bit her lip. "Oh?"

"I wasn't interested in those types of things before."

A slow grin spread over her lips. "And you are now?"

"Yes. I get to spend time with you and some of my friends. You'll have fun."

"Okay, sure."

"Good. I'll pick you up for lunch and we'll head over that way after I run a quick errand."

"Sounds good," she said, not wanting to hang up.

"Later, love."

Ugh. She hung up and stared at her phone. She needed a life. She was turning into a hormone ridden teenager. All she thought of the entire day was Xander and how he made her feel. How he treated her. If she didn't find something to do soon, she was scared he'd tire of her and she'd be left alone with nothing to keep her going.

CHAPTER SIXTEEN

Leigh ate a meatball and watched Marleen and Ginger play UNO. She'd never seen two people more into the game than them.

"Isn't this supposed to be a fun family game?" she asked, taking another bite of her meatball.

"Yeah," Marleen said and put down a plus four card.

Ginger glared at her and picked up four cards. "This is family fun, dammit."

"Uh, you two are making me feel like we're about to watch a serious wrestling match happen when one of you loses."

"She's right," Ginger sighed. "Let's take a break. I'm hungry."

Marleen gave a strange grin. "You knew I had you. But I'll let you concede defeat."

Ginger rolled her eyes. "Whatever."

They went to the food on the table and Marleen sniffed the bouquet of roses William had sent her. "These are so beautiful." She smiled at Leigh. "Don't you love them?"

"Yeah." No sense in telling either of them her troubles with William.

"There's a second set," Marleen frowned. "Your boyfriend?"

"Nah, they're from my brother, Kellan."

"Oh, I remember him."

"Yeah. He's a sweet guy and I'm sure he feels bad he's not here after my return home from my last shitty breakup."

"So, Marleen," Ginger started, cutting into a piece of chicken piccata. "Why did you leave town all those years ago?"

Leigh stared at Marleen who in turn stared at her. "My parents had a hard time being parents and they sent me to live with some family in another state."

"But you were about to graduate high school," Leigh said, frowning. "Weren't you going to go away to school anyway?"

She nodded. "That was the plan. But once I was living with my aunt in South Carolina, I realized those plans weren't going to work for me any longer."

"How did you even get into cooking?" Ginger asked and mmm'ed over her food.

Marleen grinned. "My aunt taught me how to cook and I found I really enjoyed it. So I ended up going to culinary school. I worked as a chef at different restaurants until I found my way back here."

"You're really good at it," Leigh mumbled, eating her pasta.

"What about you? What brought you back?"

"Bad breakup. I needed a change and now I'm here and don't know what I'm supposed to do."

"You were always so good with art in school," Marleen said. "I used to love seeing your paintings after school. Mrs. Gellar would display them, and I was always caught up by your use of color and the emotions in your work."

Leigh blushed. "I loved painting. I still do. In New York, I had the tiniest section by a window where I'd paint every day. It's what kept me sane."

"Hey!" Ginger sat up with a squeal. "Why don't you substitute at the elementary school for the art teacher? Or even the high school? Their art programs are not what they used to be. I'm sure you'd have fun and the kids could use someone who loves art there to teach them."

"You think?" She frowned. "I never thought of teaching."

Marleen nodded. "I never thought I'd love cooking, but here I am. Why don't you give it a try?" She squeezed Leigh's hand, rubbing her thumb across the back in a relaxing touch. "This could be great for you."

"I'll think about it," Leigh said. "It would be new and different."

"You're an amazing artist, Leigh," Marleen said. "I know your artwork will wow all those kids."

"Thanks," she mumbled, uncomfortable with all her praise.

"I'll speak to the dean of students tomorrow at the high school and the principal at the elementary school. See if they have any openings," Ginger said.

"This is a good start." Leigh glanced at the two women. Ginger had an optimistic grin on her face and Marleen's gaze was fixated on Leigh's face.

After the women had left for the night, she locked all the doors and went to her bedroom to take a hot bath. Her muscles felt tight and she needed to relax. With her claw-foot tub filling, she called the detective in New York to ask for an update.

"Detective Bradford," he answered.

"Hi, it's Leigh Hale," she said. "I'm calling to find out the status of your investigation on William Barnes."

"Ms. Hale," Detective Bradford said. "It's good to hear from you. Where are you?"

She frowned. "I told you I was heading out of town. I needed to get away from William and his scheme. I couldn't be around him and act like nothing was wrong."

"I understand, but where exactly are you?"

"What does it matter? Are you arresting him?"

"Not yet. The FBI is leading the investigation into Mr. Barnes with the District Attorney office's help. I'm no longer involved."

"Oh. Well, please give them my information in case they need to speak to me," she said. "I'll be happy to come in for an interview."

"I'll do that."

She was glad the FBI was doing the investigation into William and his Ponzi scheme. She knew he was doing bad things and if not stopped soon, people were going to find themselves broke because of him.

She carried her phone with her to the bathroom and placed it on a towel next to the tub. With candles lit, she dropped clary sage oil into the steamy water and then sat in the tub. She leaned her head back on the curve of the tub and sighed when her phone buzzed. It was Xander. She hit the speaker button and put it on the table next to the tub.

"Hi," she sighed.

"What are you doing?" he asked softly. "You sound different."

She groaned and felt her muscles loosen in the warm water. "I'm taking a bath."

"Naked?"

"That's how most people bathe." She laughed. "Yes. Naked. Very naked."

He cleared his throat. "What are you doing in the tub?"

She laughed at the rough sound of his voice. "I wasn't doing anything, but now that you're listening, I think I might like to touch myself."

He growled softly. "Do it. Let me hear you."

"Are you alone?"

"Yes. Julian just left to handle something on the casino floor. It's just me and you, love."

She nibbled on her bottom lip and groaned. "Tell me, Xander. Tell me what to do."

"Cup your breasts," he said, his voice thick with need. "Fondle your nipples. Let me hear you moan when you do it."

She slid her hands up her ribs to cup her full breasts, tugging at her nipples. She whimpered at the sting of pain. Her breaths came in short rasps. Behind her closed lids, all she saw was his face. His voice filled her head with images of him touching her.

"Yes, baby," he breathed on the phone. "Pinch your nipples. Feel me touching you. That's me, love. It's me tweaking your nipples and squeezing your tits. Fuck, Leigh. You're so beautiful. Touch your pussy for me."

She moaned, keeping one hand on her breast and sliding the other between her thighs. She lifted both legs out of the water and draped them over the sides of the tub. Then she rubbed at her pussy folds, sliding two fingers into her sex and then backing out to flick her middle finger over her clit.

"Oh, god," she gasped.

"Keep going, love. Faster," he growled. "Let me hear you come, Leigh."

She moved her finger faster, pressing hard and rubbing her clit in quick motions. A pinch and tug at her nipple and she cried out when the orgasm took her over.

Her body trembled and her pussy grasped at nothing with every wave of her climax.

"Fuck!" He growled. "I wish I were there to lick your pussy up and savor your wetness."

She sucked in harsh breaths and lay in the water, trying to slow her pulse. "I can't believe I just did that with you on the phone."

"Baby, I can't believe I'm not in my car driving there right now to finish you off," he grunted. "I should be with you. Making you come again with my cock deep inside you. I should be kissing you all over, loving every inch of your beautiful body."

Yes. Yes, he should. But she wasn't going to say that. "You've got stuff to handle, Xander. A business to run. I'm okay. I'm going to bed now."

"I'll be at the hotel for a bit. Goodnight, love," he whispered.

"Goodnight," she replied and hung up. Her heartbeat was still erratic. She'd never done phone sex before. Xander was making her do things she never thought possible. She liked it. She liked how free she felt with him. She liked that it was okay for her to try and do anything and he only cared about making her happy and nothing else.

CHAPTER SEVENTEEN

Xander hoped Leigh didn't freak out with his plan. After Ginger called him with her own thoughts on Leigh's desire to try something new, he realized she needed to be able to try going back into art without feeling pressured.

He'd always known Leigh was an overachiever, so it worried him how much she was floundering now that she was home. He needed to help her somehow. He thought he had an idea in mind.

He watched her from the driver's side, glancing out the window.

"So where are we going?" she asked, turning to face him. She gave him a dazzling smile, her green eyes bright and full of joy. That's how he always wanted to see her. The bruising had gone, and her face was back to its original creamy complexion.

"First," he said, "we're going to lunch. I think you're going to like what I have planned."

She'd worn one of the dresses he'd bought her. It was white with red polka dots and it made her look like a piece of candy. They parked outside the town bookstore.

She raised her brows and glanced at him. "What in the world are we doing here?"

He took her hand and led her inside. "You'll see."

Throughout her life in Denali Ridge, she'd loved going to this bookstore. He remembered how she'd always begged as a kid for Kellan to take her to the bookstore or for her nanny to take her. When he'd gone off to college, he remembered Kellan mentioning how she lived in the bookstore more than at home. Working there part-time to make some money while at the same time being surrounded by one of the things she loved the most. Books.

Where there would normally be reading time for kids, he'd had a table set up with lunch for them.

She gasped and glanced at the candle-lit table with rose centerpiece. "What is this?"

"Lunch," he said and watched surprise and then joy animate her features.

"This is...wow." She threw herself in his arms and kissed all over his face. "I can't tell you how special this is."

His heart beat twice as fast when he felt her happiness. "I hope you like it."

He pulled the chair back for her to sit and then sat across from her. Julian showed up a moment later, a napkin draped over his arm.

"Welcome to Denali Ridge Bookstore," Julian bowed. "I'm your waiter for today's lunch. Can I get you some drinks?"

She blinked at Julian and grinned. "Lemonade?"

"You got it. I mean," Julian cleared his throat, "yes, madam."

She giggled and turned to Xander. "You?"

"I already know what he wants," Julian said, rolling his eyes. "Water with lemon."

He left them alone. "Good help is hard to come by," Xander told her.

She laughed outright and glanced around them in awe. "How did you get this place for us for lunch?"

"The owner's a friend of mine."

She squinted as if trying to read into his words. "Right."

"It's true. He's been trying to get me to buy the place for a while now, so when I asked for this favor, he said yes hoping that me spending some time here would help me fall in love with the place."

She gaped at him. "How could you not be in love with it already?"

"I have some ideas," he told her. The biggest idea he had was for her, but he didn't want to stress her talking of money when he knew she'd lost a lot of her trust and savings investing in William Barnes' scheme.

Julian returned with their drinks and their first course. He remembered how much she loved Caesar salad from several conversations he'd had with Kellan.

"Caesar salad," she laughed, "my favorite."

"I know," Julian said. "He won't stop talking about all the stuff you like."

Leigh giggled and Xander shook his head. "I told you it's hard to find good help."

"I'll be back with your main course in a few," Julian said. "Holler if you need anything."

"You know," Leigh glanced at the sofa in the corner of the kids' reading section. "My mom hated coming here because I wanted to spend the entire day in here reading all the books. That was the first reason she got me a nanny. The second was that she just didn't have the patience to deal with someone so energetic." She grinned and pointed to a stain on the carpet. "I did that one day. I can't believe they still have the same carpet. I was drinking fruit punch and decided to throw a fit when it was time to leave."

He chuckled at the image of little Leigh throwing a tantrum. He couldn't visualize that. All he remembered of Leigh was her being the happiest, most entertaining little girl. "That doesn't sound like you."

She nodded. "I know, right? But that day, I was upset because that was the day you went on vacation with your family. You went skiing or something."

"Yeah," he laughed. "I remember that. We went to visit friends up in the mountains. I spent my time hanging out with my good friend Zain and his family. We did go skiing."

"I was so sad you'd left. And you took Kellan

with you. So I threw a fit and my poor mother didn't know how to handle it."

"Kellan always said how you loved coming here."

"Yeah. I even worked here when I was in high school." She ate her salad. "By then, I never saw you again and Kellan barely came home."

"There were some issues with him and your parents," he said. He wondered how much of the troubles between Kellan and their parents she was aware of.

"What do you mean?"

"Kellan didn't return because your father told him not to. He specifically asked him to stay away from you if he planned on leading such a dangerous life. He didn't want you growing attached to him only to one day find out he'd been killed on the job."

She stared at him, horror filling her eyes. "What?"

For the first time in his life, he hated having to tell someone the truth about her parents. "I'm sorry, love. But your parents pushed Kellan away the minute he joined the military and went on to be part of a special ops unit."

Her pain filled his heart with sorrow. He grabbed her hand on the table and squeezed. “I’m so sorry, Leigh.”

She gulped visibly. “Why?”

CHAPTER EIGHTEEN

Leigh couldn't believe what Xander had just told her. Her parents pushed Kellan out the door and told him not to return? It made no sense. They loved her brother.

"Your father was a control freak," Xander told her. "I'm sorry to be the one who tells you this, but he wanted your brother to go into banking and stay local. To start a business with him and grow the Hale name." He pushed his salad plate away. "When Kellan told them he was going into the military, your mother freaked out. Your father basically disowned him. They told him to limit his visits to as few as possible."

She frowned and shook her head. "But my parents loved Kellan. He was all they ever spoke of to anyone. My dad didn't even bat an eye when I went into banking trying to make him happy. All he ever spoke of was Kellan. His son."

"Leigh, I'm sorry. When he went to college and was recruited, your parents told him that he was only allowed to come over when you weren't around. That they didn't want you growing more attached to him."

The pain in her chest grew with each of his words. She believed him. How many times had she wondered why Kellan never came home? Why he showed up when she was off at some camp or activity. Why didn't he write or call her?

"It didn't matter what they told him," she said, softly. "I have always loved my brother. And limiting our contact only hurt us, but it didn't stop me from loving him."

"I know, love. Kellan knew that, too. That's why when your parents passed away, he wasn't sure how to reestablish a relationship with you."

She gasped. "And that's when I told him I was moving to New York." She brushed a long strand of red hair behind her ear. "He wanted me to stay here, but I refused. I secretly felt that he'd left me for so long that there was no reason for me to be here."

"He hated staying away from you, but he did what your parents asked out of respect for them."

This was new and eye opening. "I had no idea."

He nodded, a grim look on his face. "I figured. I know Kellan would never tell you that your parents had pulled him away from you. But you needed to know that he's always cared about you. Always made you his priority."

"Thank you," she said, realizing how much she needed to hear that. She'd always felt like Kellan wasn't interested in her life. Like she'd just been a bother to him. Now she knew better.

"I'm back," Julian said. "I hope you're hungry because this looks great and if you're not hungry I am, so just let me know."

She laughed and watched him remove their salad plates and replace them with their entrees. She had a plate of grilled shrimp and steak with broccolini.

"Somebody really did their homework," she said, raising her brows high. "This is one of my favorites."

"I know," Julian said again. "He likes steak and potatoes more than vegetables, but he is forced to eat them if he goes to see Belinda."

"Your mom is a great cook," she said. "I'd eat anything she makes."

"We all do," Julian laughed and left.

They ate their food and she told him more stories of working at the bookstore. She'd loved this place. It was the one location she'd always felt at home. When the owner started giving painting classes, she'd been even more excited to spend time there. Her parents hadn't minded that she was never home. They were too busy going out on their boat with their retired friends.

Julian returned with coffee and dessert. He brought them fried cheesecake and she groaned just listening to him tell how it had been prepared.

The first bite of her cheesecake and she moaned. "This is so much better than what I imagined."

She opened her eyes to catch Xander staring at her lips. His eyes flashed and a sense of being prey under the watch of a predator took her over. He licked his lips and stared at her mouth. "Can I get a taste?"

She nodded jerkily but was completely unprepared for him to pull her chair toward him and cup the back of her head, bringing her face to his. Their lips plastered together, and she moaned at the invasion of his tongue into her mouth. A soft growl sounded from him. Desire blossomed in her core, heating her blood and making her wiggle in her seat.

The kiss deepened and pulled them both into a desire neither wanted to let go of. She clung to his shirt, her nails raking over the back of his neck. She nibbled on his lips and gripped his hand in hers. Another growl sounded from him and he pulled away.

"We need to stop," he said, breathing heavily. "Before Julian returns to find me fucking you on this table."

She blinked, trying hard to push away the desire for more of his touch. More of his kisses. But it was hard. All her mind wanted was more time with Xander. More of him. Only him. The need for him grew with every waking moment. But they'd yet to discuss long-term.

For all she knew, they were just dating, and he'd eventually tire of her. That thought alone was like a bucket of cold water on her system. She sat back and let out several short breaths. Xander had gotten into her blood. And she wasn't sure she wanted him out.

CHAPTER NINETEEN

After their amazing lunch, he took her to his friend Ryan's house for couples' night. Ryan was a tiger shifter and his wife, Parker, was human. The other couple was a little different than what she expected. Two guys, Dean and Gavin, both wolf shifters, and their mate, Jade.

Jade and Parker's cousin Balgair was there with his husband, Jay. He was a really sweet guy with a better sense of style than Leigh. Maybe not Parker, though. She looked ready to rock the runway in her pencil skirt and heeled sandals.

All of them looked so happy. Surprisingly, even the threesome appeared to get along well for it being two men sharing one woman. She'd never met other shifters, so she wasn't sure how the sharing worked, but it must be working for them because Jade was glowing with happiness. Same with Parker. Both women looked like they were very happy. Balgair seemed to be totally obsessed with his husband, and it was really cute to see his husband giving him adoring glances all the time.

"Leigh," Parker called her to the kitchen. "Come on over here and hang with us."

Leigh went into the kitchen and watched Parker take covers off the food containers and line them on the kitchen island like a big buffet.

"Are you hungry?" Jade asked. "There's a ton of food."

"And not because either of them cooked," Balgair said. "Dean's mom had her chef make everything."

Jade grinned. "It's true. She actually wanted to do it. She said she got to stay with her grandson for a few hours and we deserved some couples' time."

Balgair handed Leigh a glass of wine. "Here you go, honey. You look like you need it."

She laughed and shook her head. "Sorry. I'm just not used to being around so many people. I didn't even go on outings when I lived in New York."

"I love New York," Parker and Jade said in unison.

Balgair chuckled. "Doesn't everyone?"

Leigh sighed. "Not me. I was in over my head in New York. There were just too many people. Everyone was always in a rush. I ended up getting severe anxiety dealing with my demanding job and the city itself."

"I can understand that," Jade said. "How are you coping now that you're living in Denali Ridge?"

"And what we really want to know," Balgair asked, "is when you and Xander are making it official."

She blinked. "What?"

"Your mating," Parker replied, elbowing her cousin. "You behave. She hasn't been here for thirty minutes and you're already pressing her for a wedding date."

"I, uh," she frowned. "I don't know that's where Xander wants to go."

They all looked at each other and burst into giggles.

"Honey," Jade handed her a mini crab cake on a stick. "He's a shifter. That's where they all want to go. Once a shifter finds his mate, it's only a matter of time before he wants to be mated." She glanced down at her wedding rings. "Most of the time, they'll want to get married, too, to cover all bases." She laughed. "Make sure you're his in every way possible."

"But Xander hasn't mentioned any of that." He'd only discussed how glad he was she was home and the joke of her being his wife. Sure, they'd had amazing sex, but none of that equaled to a long-term relationship, much less marriage.

"He might just be giving you time to get to know him," Balgair said and popped a mini crab cake in his mouth.

"How do you know him?" Parker asked.

"He's my brother's best friend. I've known Xander most of my life. When I was four or five, I asked him to marry me. I always had this obsession with him and his smile."

"Aww," Jade sighed. "You asked him when you were that young?"

She snorted. "Yeah. He showed up the other day demanding his wife. He was kidding, of course."

"Sure he was," Parker said. "Are you in love with him?"

"Parker!" Jade exclaimed. "You can't ask her that."

Balgair raised his brows. "Why not? Are you?"

Leigh's stomach knotted but she wasn't one to lie. She was beyond in love with Xander. She'd never not been in love with him. What she had been was in denial for a long time.

"You don't have to answer that," Jade told her. "Xander's a great guy."

Parker nodded. "He is. And I'm sure that soon he'll tell you how much he wants you to be his mate."

Anxiety grew in Leigh's chest. What if he didn't? What if the reason he wasn't discussing mating or marriage was because he just wasn't interested?

"You look like you're gonna be sick," Jade said, rubbing her arm. "Don't think the worst, Leigh." She gave her a worried look. "I was in your shoes a year ago. I didn't believe that Dean and Gavin could really love me and want to be with me, but they did. They do."

Parker nodded. "I was there, too. It's hard when you're mated to a shifter because we humans have so many insecurities, and we don't know if what we feel is what they feel. Meanwhile in their minds, we're all married and should be having children. They're that decisive.

"It's because they have this sense that tells them you're the right one for them. They don't question it. They just know." She sighed. "We don't have that. We just have our feelings. And those are always a mess when it comes to figuring out how to admit being in love."

"Humans are definitely more complex," Balgair said. "But it doesn't have to be. Do you love him? Yes? Okay. If he's with you here, we know he loves you and wants you to be his mate. There is no in between. He either wants you or he doesn't. You don't ever have to worry about Xander lying to you about his feelings. He won't. Just ask him. He will tell you."

She'd never thought to do that. Not that she knew much about shifters, but it was something she'd give a try.

They ate and drank and then everyone went to the main living area where an easel had been set up with markers.

"What are we playing?" Leigh asked Xander as he pulled her onto his lap.

"Pictionary," Jade replied. "Couples *Dirty*

Pictionary. The couple with the most right in the least amount of time wins."

Leigh glanced at Xander and watched his features turn determined. "We can win this, Leigh."

She chuckled and nodded. "It's in the bag."

"Aww, they're so cute," Balgair said. "You're going down. All of you."

Well, damn. This was a competitive bunch.

Up first was Team Balgair. Balgair's husband, Jay, got to draw while he got to guess. The moment that timer was flipped over, Jay began scribbling lines furiously.

"A couple having sex," Balgair yelled.

Everyone chuckled. "Stick people having sex," Balgair shouted. "People having sex in a car. A car." He opened his eyes wide. "Sex on the beach!"

"Time!" Jade yelled.

Balgair's husband wiped his brow and sighed. "Right on time, too."

"Sex on the beach is right," Jade said. "All right, Parker and Ryan, you're up."

Parker stood by the easel and blew Ryan a kiss. "You've got this, babe."

He gave a nod and winked at her. "I know."

Parker glanced at her card and then waited for Jade to flip the timer. "Go!"

Parker started drawing what looked like a woman.

"Boobs," Ryan called out. "Sexy boobs, big boobs, little boobs?"

Parker glared at him and drew the bottom half of the woman.

"Big ass," Ryan chuckled. "Anal? Anal sex. Dual penetration?"

Then she drew what looked like a penis on the female.

Ryan cocked his head and gasped. "Strap-on!"

"Yes!" Parker squealed and ran into his arms, just as the timer went off.

"A few seconds on the lead," Jade told them. "Okay, it's our turn, guys." Jade picked up a card and laughed before putting it back down and picking up a marker. Parker put the timer on.

"Go!"

Jade started drawing what looked like two circles.

"Coming in her eyes," Gavin yelled. Dean slapped him on the side and shook his head.

"Nipples? Big nipples? Man nipples?" Dean hollered.

Jade then drew what looked like a penis between the two circles.

"Balls? Man balls? Horny balls?" Gavin continued.

Jade grabbed a blue marker and filled in the circles.

"Blue balls!" Dean yelled.

"Time!"

Jade bounced and jumped on Dean's lap, kissing both men. "Blue balls is right."

"Parker and Ryan are in the lead, followed by Jade, Dean, and Gavin and then Balgair and Jay. You're up, Leigh and Xander."

Leigh was super competitive and wanted to win in the least amount of time. That would give them a good lead as they continued on the game.

"You draw," he said, squeezing her hand. "We've got this."

She stood and picked up a card and laughed. Then she put it down and waited until Jade gave her the go. She glanced around, seeing the couples holding each other and laughing or kissing. The she looked at Xander. Her heart filled with so much love, it almost choked her. She wished that moment could last. That things could go farther between them.

"Ready?" Jade asked, bringing her back to the present. "Go!"

Leigh immediately set to draw an animal. She did a basic sketch and made sure to show the humps. Then she drew the feet large and circled the toe. Xander wasn't yelling out answers like the others. Instead he waited until she finished her sketch.

"Camel toe," he laughed.

She jumped up and down and ran over to hop on his lap. Then she kissed him all over his face and hugged him hard.

"Camel toe is right," Jade groaned. "That was fast." She glanced at Parker and Balgair. "They have a big lead."

Balgair waved a hand as if it was no big deal. "I'm winning tonight. Last time, Parker took the win. I'm not going home empty-handed."

An hour later, Balgair went home with dessert, because Leigh and Xander won. They had the best time and her sketches were, according to everyone, the best ones to understand.

"Your prize for tonight," Jade handed Leigh a black bag. "Enjoy."

They went to her home after that.

CHAPTER TWENTY

Leigh loved the feel of Xander under her when she woke. It was the middle of the night, but she wanted him. She'd always want him.

"Mmm," she moaned. Her body lay half over his warm one. He was so big and strong. She loved how small and cared for he made her feel. She trailed her hand down his abs and wrapped it around his cock. "You're so hard. I like that."

A soft growl sounded from him. "Fuck, Leigh."

"Mmm," she moaned. "I think that's a good idea."

"What is?"

"Fucking," she sighed.

He groaned at the stroke of her hand on his

hardness. She loved touching him. She gripped him tight in her hand.

"God, Leigh!" He growled. "I'm not going to hold on for long."

She squeezed him even tighter.

"Babe, you don't have to," he choked out.

"I know," she whispered, kissing her way down his abs. "I want to."

Her lips hovered over him. He pushed her long hair out of the way and cupped her face, so she'd meet his stare. She stared into his blazing hungry eyes. She licked her lips, glanced down at his cock and then back at him. "I'm starving."

"Yeah?"

"Oh, yeah," she whispered.

"I've got some things you can munch on in the kitchen."

She licked the tip of his dick and grinned at the way he sucked air hard.

"I found something I want. I bet it's delicious." She licked a circle around his shaft, rolling her tongue repeatedly up to the head.

"*Fuuuuck,*" he rumbled. He twined his fingers in her hair, gripping the long strands in his fists. "Suck me into your mouth, love. I want to watch."

She felt his muscles tense. She sucked her lips tight around his cock.

"Oh, baby. Just like that."

She moaned deep in her throat.

He urged her to take more of him into her mouth by lifting his hips and pushing down her throat. "I want you to ride me next, love."

Her head bobbed over him, up and down. Fuck. He tasted so good. He was so big. All she kept picturing was his hot hardness inside her, stroking her insides and making her come.

"Come here, my love." He tugged her face off his cock. She met his gaze and gave him a long and slow final lick. He grunted when she pulled him from her lips. "You're too good at that."

"I aim to please," she grinned and crawled forward, rubbing her breasts on his pecs. The touch of her skin on his made her blood sizzle. "I can keep pleasing you."

"You're about to please the hell out of me, babe," he said with a smile.

She straddled him, grasped his cock with one hand and licked her lips. "Let's see how much you like it."

He stared deep into her eyes. "I already love it. All of you."

She moaned and wiggled over his hardness. He was so hot, and her pussy was slick and wet. "Xander, I need you."

"Ride me," he ordered, his words a mere growl.

Leigh lifted and placed the head of his cock at her pussy entrance. She felt him slide in slowly. She wanted him to claim her. To take her. She was his and she knew it. Did he know it?

Xander bit his fingers into her waist and pulled her down at the same time he lifted his hips off the bed, impaling her with his cock.

"Oh, God!" she screamed, her pussy fluttering and clamping around his shaft.

"Fucking hell that feels good," he snarled. "You feel perfect."

He didn't wait for her to adjust. Instead, he grabbed her ass cheeks and forced her body forward to rock over him.

"Mine!"

She moaned and raked her nails on his chest. Leaning down, she nuzzled his lips and licked his jaw.

With another rock on his cock, she watched him pull something from under his pillow. It was a pocket rocket. A slow grin spread over her lips. One of the toys they'd won earlier in their black bag. He pressed a button and a soft buzzing sounded along with her hard breathing.

She groaned, pinching her nipples and watching him press the toy on her clit when she rocked back.

"Oh, my," she gasped.

The little toy vibrated against her clit when she rocked forward, but he pulled it back when she wiggled back.

"Don't stop," she panted. "Please."

"I don't plan to," he said gruffly. "Not until I watch you come on my dick." She was no longer rocking but lifting and dropping on his dick.

She was so close to coming. Her body shook. It was hard to move away from the toy and every touch of the vibrating toy on her clit made her jerk.

"Oh my God!" She dropped her head forward, her body tensing and every move harder for her.

"That's it, love. Take my cock." He pressed the vibrator on her clit. "Keep that tight pussy sucking me," he groaned.

She ground her pussy down into his pelvis and the vibrator. She came fast and hard, her body shuddering and her pussy clamping tight around his dick. A loud moan fell from her lips followed by a much louder scream as a second orgasm rushed her.

A loud growl sounded from him. His cock pulsed in her channel, filling her with his cum. It was fucking amazing.

She fell on his chest, struggling to catch her breath. He rubbed his hand up and down her back and kissed her forehead.

"You sure know how to wake me up."

She chuckled and glanced up to meet his gaze. "I really woke up for a snack."

He raised his brows. "Oh, really?"

She shook her head and kissed his chest. "Not that kind of snack. I want food, lion man."

"Your wish is my command, love," he said. "But you're going to have to let me out of bed to get it."

She groaned and felt him harden inside her. "In a minute."

CHAPTER TWENTY-ONE

Xander hated leaving Leigh's bed. Once they were mated, everything else would have to wait. Maybe it would be a good time to step back from the businesses and pass the major duties to his second-in-command so he could focus on his soon-to-come family.

He headed to the buffet to have breakfast with Julian and catch up on casino happenings.

"Had a high roller in last night," Julian told him. "East Coast accent. Haughty. I could tell he was an asshole by looking at him."

Xander raised a brow. "Higher roller than normal, I'm guessing."

"He wasn't worried about any losses, of which he didn't have many."

"Cheating?" Xander asked.

"I couldn't see it, but it had to be something. Nobody is that fucking lucky."

"Is he staying in the hotel?" If so, perhaps he could invite the man to lunch or spot him a table with electronic surveillance that messes with any transmissions coming in and out of the room. They could see how lucky the man was then.

"Noticed your SUV wasn't in the drive this morning," Julian commented. "Stay the night somewhere else?"

"With my future alpha mate," he said, not happy that his second would imply anything else.

Julian lifted his hands, palms out. "That's what I'm getting at. Chill, man."

Xander slammed back his orange juice. "Yeah, sorry. This shit with her ex is getting to me. I'm constantly worried the man will show up. Find out anything more about him yet?"

"Our guy is looking. The man's name is well known, so if he's pulling a fast one, it'll be the crime of the decade."

He wondered what Leigh saw that made her think her ex was dirty. Not that he minded since it made her come home. She was a banker, so she probably knew what she was looking at.

"Oh," Julian said, "one of *the ladies* needs to speak with you today."

"Which one?" he asked.

"Room 109."

"Staci," Xander replied.

"Yeah, can't keep up with their names as well as you."

"Don't worry about it. Your job is just to make sure they stay safe. You never know if your mate may be one we help."

Julian snorted. "I doubt that. I'm not as lucky as you."

"Lucky?" he said. "How am I lucky?"

"Are you kidding? You've got the money, looks, mate, perfect parents. What else could you possibly want?"

"My own family." That came out more seriously than he intended. It shut his friend down, though.

"Well, you got your mate. It'll come quickly."

"I don't have her yet. I've known my mate her entire life, but she never knew I was a shifter."

Julian's brow buried under his bangs. "Seriously? How'd she manage that?"

He shrugged. "Nobody told her. I don't think she knows a thing about shifters."

"You think she'll freak when you shift?" his friend asked.

He shook his head. "No, she saw my lion when it took out the burglars."

"Right," Julian said. "Forgot about that." After a moment, he said, "So what's the problem? She's not afraid of your lion. What else is there?"

He sat back and sighed. "I don't know what it is. But I feel something is holding her back."

"Oh, you're confused because she wanted to go back to her own home instead of staying with you."

"She was safe at my place. I could watch over her all day and night—"

"Stop right there," his second said, lifting a hand, "that's the problem."

"What?" he asked, not grasping what could possibly be wrong.

"You're smothering her."

"What?"

Julian nodded. "You're too much for her to take. Back off a bit to let her think for herself and realize how much she likes being with you. If you're always there, then she won't know how unhappy she is without you."

"Is that how it works?" Xander asked. "Don't promise her a rose garden?"

"Along with the sunshine, there's got to be a little rain sometime. You got it."

He wiped a hand down his face. "Yeah, okay. Maybe." He hated the idea of her not being with him. What if her ex came after her? Should he be worried about that?

CHAPTER TWENTY-TWO

Leigh stretched under her warm covers. When she reached behind her, she felt paper where a body should've been. Damn. She brought the note to her and read the note from Xander.

My love,

I hate to leave you this morning. You looked so beautiful and delicious at the same time. But I needed to stop by the casino for a bit. I will call later.

Thinking of you,

X

. . .

Leigh smashed the paper to her chest. Could he be more perfect? She flipped off the covers and took a quick shower before putting on leggings and a tee. She danced down the hallway like she used to do when she was a kid, pretending it was her spotlight moment on stage where everyone had their eyes on her.

What a great day to be alive. That was until she got to the coffeemaker and realized she still didn't have the miracle java in the house. She sighed, dropping her chin to her chest. She needed to find her shoes for another trip to Ginger's. If she did anything when she got home, it would be grocery shopping.

Ten minutes later, she stood in line behind a few others who obviously didn't have a stash of coffee at home either.

"Leigh Hale?" she heard behind her. She turned to see one of her elementary teachers. The woman had aged, but she still looked the same.

"Mrs. Portel, oh my gosh. How are you?" Leigh stepped out of line to hug the older lady.

"I'm good. Retiring after this school year. Final-ly." Mrs. Portel laughed.

"Wow," Leigh said, "you've been teaching forev-er." The woman laughed again, and Leigh realized what she'd said may have been a smidge nonpolitically correct. "I'm mean, yes, finally." Her cheeks heated.

The teacher waved her hand through the air. "I know what you meant, no worries. What brings you back to town?"

With both her parents gone, there wasn't anything here for her. Well, almost nothing.

"I'm back for vacation time. I needed to get out of the big city," she said, hoping that lie was believable. "Maybe do some painting. A lot of sleeping."

"You are still painting?" Portel asked.

She nodded. "Whenever I can."

"You had such fantastic talent in high school. I remember yours were some of the best art I've seen."

"Oh, thank you." She wasn't expecting such praise for something she did so long ago that, in reality, wasn't all that good.

"Our art teacher is out this week. Would you like to be a guest artist? I think the kids would love it."

Whoa, that came out of nowhere. She thought about it for a moment. Ginger had said something about teaching, but she hadn't thought about it yet.

"You know, I'd love to do that. What do you want me to do and when?"

"Anything you want. And *today*."

Yikes! Could she be prepared that quickly? "Don't you need permission from the principal or someone before I can show up?"

Mrs. Portel smiled. "I am the principal now."

She liked the idea. Maybe if someone had shown her the craft, and not only finger painting, at a younger age, she may have started sooner and made something of herself.

Portel continued. "You'll have forty-five minutes. It'll be second graders at Denali Ridge Peak."

"Oh," Leigh had gone to a different primary school. The Peak hadn't opened until she was in seventh grade. It was on the other side of town where those who lived closer to the casinos went.

They made final plans with both paying for coffee and waving goodbye. Leigh rushed home to see if her old painting supplies were still there. On the way, her phone rang. She answered through her car's speaker system.

"Hey, babe." Xander's sexy voice rolled with deep bass. Damn, it made her hot just hearing it.

"Hey, back, big boy. Is the office under control?" she asked.

"Almost. There are ruffians and heathens all over the place. And most of them have my same last name."

Leigh laughed. That was one thing Xander could always do—cheer her up. He made her smile just by being around. She couldn't believe how she completely put him from her mind after she hit New York.

"What are your plans for today? You free this afternoon?" he asked.

"Actually, I'm substituting for an art teacher today and tomorrow. I saw one of my past teachers at Ginger's this morning."

He chuckled. "Still haven't gone grocery shopping then?"

She huffed. "Like I've had time. Somebody's been hogging me to themselves."

"Oink, oink," he replied. "What time and where?"

She filled him in on the discussion, passing the Main Street Diner's empty parking lot. They wouldn't open until just before lunch.

"You know," he said, "I miss you already."

Her heart melted. "I am sorta cold without you wrapped around me."

"Baby, you were hot as hell, soaking my cock as I pounded in and out of you last night." A thrill ran through her at his seductive words. William had never said anything like that to her. In fact, he never said much at all except *spread your legs now*. Then after a minute or two, she could roll back over.

With Xander, there was rolling, but it wasn't by herself. She had to get him off the phone or she would experience her second time of phone sex, but this time in a car. She passed a black sedan parked along the side of the road a few houses from hers then pulled into her drive. A person sat inside and hadn't gotten out yet. She took her time, waiting to see if he went to one of the homes. Nope. He didn't move.

She hurried inside to see what supplies she'd have to purchase and make a plan that second graders would enjoy. She wanted to make it fun and memorable. In her excited haste, she almost forgot to drink her coffee.

Time whipped past and she found herself having to drive around a bit to find the school. She had a general idea where it was but hadn't been there. Finally, she pulled in and parked and somehow Xander was right beside her when she looked through the passenger window. He hopped out of his SUV, bent down, and pressed his face to her window. His nose flattened and lips spread out.

She burst out in laughter for a long moment. She was still laughing when he walked around to her side of the car and opened her door.

His eyes rolled. "It wasn't that funny."

She laughed harder at his adorable expression then dropped the visor to wipe her eyes and check her French beret that was part of her costume. He offered a hand to assist her out. He pulled her into a passionate kiss that curled her toes and made her cheeks rosy.

"Xander, someone might see," she said.

He nibbled her earlobe. "That's the whole point, love."

She smacked his arm, laughing, and pulled back. "Help me get my stuff out." She popped the trunk then grabbed her purse.

From the back, Xander hollered. "Holy shit. What are you doing with all this stuff? I thought you were showing kids how to paint, not decorating a movie set."

She rolled her eyes and pointed to the big plastic container. "Just carry it inside. You'll see." She bit her lip, trying not to laugh and give away her surprise.

She carried in the easel and stretched canvas, watching Xander's arms and back muscles roll under his taut shirt. She couldn't wait to have another bite of that. Mrs. Portel met them at the entrance to the school.

"Alpha," Portel said, "nice to see you."

Leigh glanced between the two. "You know each other?"

Xander smiled at the older woman. "Of course. Mrs. Portel has been our principal for many years. We're going to miss her when she retires."

That was surprising, but she wasn't sure why. Was Mrs. Portal a shifter? How many people in town did she know who were part of Xander's pride and never knew?

The elder showed them to the art room so they could set up for the class. Easel and canvas ready, Leigh pulled a shirt from the plastic container and tossed it to Xander. "Put this on," she said.

He held it up, letting it unfold. "Why is there a beetle imprinted on the front?"

"Just put it on," she said trying to hide her

smile. His eyes narrowed at her. Damn, he was smoldering hot.

The bell rang and kids started filing in. Many faces burst into wide smiles when seeing Xander. Several called out *alpha* and waved. Many sat on the floor, starstruck with mouth gaping, staring at him. The small room filled, whispering and pointing at the alpha. Well, she had their attention, sorta.

"Allo, bonjour, everyone," she said. "That means hello in French where painting is famous." She kept up a faux accent that wasn't French or anything else, getting a raised brow from Xander.

"My name is Lee-lee, and this is my assis*tont,* Bug."

The kids screamed out laughing. Twitters and whispers of "She called Alpha a bug!" and "The alpha is a bug!" flew through the young audience.

Her heart melt when he blushed. Mrs. Portel laughed at that. "Not often we see that, Alpha."

He lifted Leigh's hand to his lips and kissed her fingers. The kids stared slack-jawed while she blushed. He smiled. "It all depends on who is speaking, Mrs. Portel."

"I see," the principal replied with a nod.

She saw what? Leigh wondered. She slapped his

hand holding hers. "Not in front of the children, Bug." After the kids settled, Leigh continued.

"I am here today to teach you how easy it is to paint." She put a hand on the stand. "Who knows what this is called?"

The kids looked at each other, nobody volunteering an answer until a little blonde raised her hand. "An easel," she replied.

"Yes," Leigh said, clasping her hands. "Bug, please write that on the board."

Xander snapped to attention and snatched up a dry-erase marker and wrote *e-a-s-l-e* on the whiteboard.

Leigh picked up her brush. "Now—" the small blonde raised her hand. "Yes," Leigh called on her.

"I think Alpha, I mean Bug, spelled it wrong."

She and Xander turned to look at the word written in blue. Alpha winked at the child. "Just testing you all." He wiped off the last two letters and wrote *e-l*. Leigh rolled her eyes. *Testing my ass.*

Leigh lifted her brush. "What is this?" The kids yelled out the answer and he wrote *brush* on the board. Then from the plastic container, she picked up her palette. "What is this?"

That one stumped them. She got guesses of

round board with a hole, paddle, and *the thing you put a cake on.*

"Close," she replied. "It's a palette." She turned to Xander and he jumped and turned to the board. He wrote *p-a-l,* then froze. He put a second letter *l* then erased it quickly. Then he put an *e-t* and turned around and smiled. PALET.

Leigh put her hand to her mouth and whispered. "It has two *t*'s." Without missing a beat, he flipped around and added a letter *t* to the end. Some of the kids giggled. PALETT.

She cleared her throat and covered her smile. "Two *e*'s." Repeating his move, he squeezed a skinny *e* between the existing *e* and *t*. There were a few more giggles. PALEETT.

"No," she whispered. "One before and after the *t*'s." Most of the class was laughing. He huffed and erased the whole thing and wrote PALETTE.

Leigh clapped. "That's right." The children joined in the fun. "Everybody tell Bug how good he's doing." Cheers and applause echoed in the room. Xander, Bug, took a bow.

By the time the bell rang ending class, her canvas was filled with painted lions, camels, and rose petals. And one bug. When the kids were gone, all saying bye to Bug, Mrs. Portel asked if they could come tomorrow, too. She wanted to bring her camera to take a picture for the school website.

When she and Xander were back at her car, she asked him, "You really knew how to spell palette, didn't you?"

"Of course," he smiled, "and every one of those kids will, too." He pressed her against her car. She felt his cock inflating like a balloon on a helium tank.

She rubbed her mound against his hard-on. "We could be giving the kids an eye full. That's probably a no-no."

He groaned and laid his head on her shoulder. "You're such a tease."

She laughed. "Me? I didn't drag you over her to press me against the car."

"Only because I beat you to it."

She laughed and kissed him again. Suddenly he pulled away, looking at his watch. "Hey, I need to stop by the office for a bit. I'll call you later. I want to see you again tonight." He gave her a peck on the cheek and hurried to his SUV and drove off.

CHAPTER TWENTY-THREE

Leigh was flying high. Never had she felt this happy with William. That man spent thousands of dollars on dinners, jewelry, shows, and things. Yet Xander had bought her a cup of coffee and a couple lunches.

Speaking of lunch, her stomach growled. She thought she and Xander would eat a late lunch after the class, but that wasn't going to happen. When she turned onto her road, she saw an old car in her driveway. Her heart skipped until she realized William wouldn't drive such a vehicle. And the black car was still there.

When she got closer, Marleen got out of the vehicle and waved at her. Leigh deflated with a large breath. She parked next to her new friend and got out of her car.

"Hey, Leigh," Marleen said, coming around with a huge smile on her face and giving her a hug longer than normal. Marleen pushed back, keeping her hands on her upper arms. "How are you doing? You are glowing."

Leigh laughed. "I am happy. I just spent an hour teaching second graders about painting."

"You like teaching then?" her friend asked.

"It was fun, but I have to say that Xander really stole the show."

"Xander? What's he doing with you?" Marleen's smile waivered.

Doing with me? "I guess we're seeing each other."

Marleen walked away to the other side of her car and opened the back door. She pulled out two huge baskets. Leigh hurried over to help her.

"What have you brought over?" Leigh asked, breathing deeply and loving the smell.

"I noticed you had no food, so I thought I'd come by and feed you."

"Thank you, Marleen." She'd been in New York for so long that she'd forgotten how small-town living was like. Neighbors helped neighbors without being asked.

Marleen handed a carrier to her. "This basket has chicken, mashed potatoes, green beans, and chocolate cake, and yours has water and wine."

Tears rimmed her eyes. It had been forever since she felt like someone really cared about her. "Marleen, I don't know what to say..."

"Well, I say let's go in and eat before it all gets cold."

Leigh laughed and pulled her keys from her purse. She'd get her painting supplies later. Food was more important at the time.

At the kitchen table, Marleen pulled out container after container. From her basket, Leigh lifted out two bottles of white wine—one with the cork stuck in and the other unopened—and several water bottles.

Marleen joined her in the kitchen. "How about you get the plates and silverware and I'll pour the wine."

"Wine already?" she asked.

Her friend shrugged. "It's four o'clock. Kinda early, but it goes so much better with chicken than anything else." Marleen leaned toward her. "I put it in the recipe, too. Delish."

"All right," she agreed. "Glass of white wine, please." She set two wine glasses on the counter then grabbed dishes and forks. When all was prepared, they sat to eat. Marleen opened the chicken container and the best smell Leigh had smelled in a long time made her mouth water.

"God, Marleen, you are a fabulous cook. I could learn a lot from you."

Her friend chuckled. "Anytime. I love it." With plates loaded, Leigh dug in. She hadn't had comfort food like this in years. She'd forgotten what she was missing.

Marleen pulled skin from her piece. "You've always had such beautiful skin. So creamy."

Nobody had ever told her that. "Thank you," she replied, feeling a bit self-conscious. "I'm lucky to inherit my mother's complexion."

"Are your parents still in town?" her friend asked.

"No. They both passed away several years ago. They had me late in life. What about yours?"

Marleen took a big gulp of wine. "My dad died, and Mom moved into the senior living community so she wouldn't have to mow the yard."

Leigh laughed. "I understand that. Xander came over to mow my yard."

Marleen's head snapped up. "Xander, the alpha of the lions, mowed your grass?"

She nodded. "What a sight was that to see." She fanned herself and Marleen gave her a half smile.

"Are you two dating?"

Leigh felt her heart lighten. "Yes, I guess we are. I've never been so happy." Her friend turned quiet and picked at her chicken. "Marleen, why did you get silent? What's wrong?"

Marleen set her fork down. "You know he's a lion shifter?"

Leigh nodded. "Just recently."

"So you don't know much about them?" Marleen asked.

"I know they are super strong and can shift into big-ass lions."

"They can smell lies and the emotions of others, but that's not what I'm getting at." Leigh waited for the woman to continue. "They are vicious animals, Leigh. They caught a hyena cheating. They dragged him back to the office and he never came back out to the casino floor."

That didn't seem right. Xander had killed the burglars in her home. But that was justified. Cheating didn't justify death.

"I guess you haven't been around long enough to know about Xander's exploits."

Concern crept into her mind. "What do you mean?"

"I hate to be the one to tell you this, but," she sighed. "You know the pride owns the casinos and hotels, right?" Again, she nodded. "Well, when I worked part-time in the kitchen, I heard and saw a lot of things most people don't know."

Dread filled her. What kind of things had he done? Couldn't be as bad as her ex—stealing life savings from unsuspecting, hardworking people. "Like what?"

"There are rooms on the first floor where he keeps women locked in."

She gasped. "Why? Are you sure?"

"I delivered room service to one of them. When she opened the door, I saw she had a bloody lip and dark eye. And she had on very little clothing. I asked if she was okay, and she told me she couldn't talk about it."

"What happened to her?" Why would someone who was beat up not want help?

"Different men are seen going down the hallway, then sometime later walking out. Xander visits them often."

"I don't understand," Leigh said.

Marleen grabbed her hand and rubbed her

thumb over the back like she did the last time she was there. "Leigh, he's a sex addict. Those women are who he fucks when the urge hits him. Maybe one, maybe all three at the same time."

Leigh sat back like she'd been slapped. "Why hasn't someone told the police?"

"Because all the employees know he'll find out who and kill them very painfully."

"No," she didn't believe it, "that can't be right."

"Think about it," her friend continued, "Has he said he needs to stop by the office for a bit or something has come up at the casino for a bit?"

Looking back, yeah, there had been times when he had to suddenly leave. It happened today when they were kissing at the school. She told him they couldn't make out in public, then he suddenly had to leave. There were other times, too.

"Also, new women are there constantly."

"What about the ones already there?"

Marleen shrugged. "Nobody sees them leave. They just disappear. Employees have noticed that when Julian goes for a visit, that's when they vanish."

A coldness seeped into her chest. Julian was the one who took care of the dead bodies and blood of the men who broke into her home.

She asked, "Has he done anything else?"

"Envelopes filled with money come in and go straight to his office. They say he steals from the company to furnish his extravagant lifestyle."

Leigh lit up like a volcano ready to spew. He was just as bad as William. Disgust chilled her heart.

Seemed Xander had changed a lot since his school years when he was caring and moral. And just like with William, she was sucked right into his scheme.

Marleen reached in her purse hanging on the chair. "If I were you, I get one of these." She lifted a big handgun. "This is a Glock. It will take out anything, including shifters. It was made for self-defense. It's saved my life several times. I don't go anywhere without it anymore."

Leigh reached across the table and took the woman's hand in hers. Marleen froze, staring at their joined hands. "Marleen, put the gun down. Please." When her friend continued to stare, she snapped her fingers on her other hand, bringing her visitor out of her daze. Marleen set her weapon on the table.

"Sorry," her friend said. "It's been a long time since anyone has touched me with love."

It wasn't what she'd call love, but she didn't want to argue semantics now. "Marleen, where did you go our senior year of school?"

The woman's eyes met her, red as if ready to cry, but there were no tears. "I went to Hell, Leigh. Straight into Hell." Marleen lifted her glass of wine. "Finish your drink and I'll refill them. We'll need more than one to get us through this."

Leigh downed what was left in her glass and handed it to Marleen who went into the kitchen and poured the corked bottle that had been open into Leigh's glass, then the other bottle into hers. The first bottle wasn't empty. Why did they have different wines?

She was about to ask when Marleen said, "I fell in love with you our sophomore year."

Leigh took a big gulp, then all thoughts about wine flew from her head.

CHAPTER TWENTY-FOUR

Marleen sat at her idol's table, terror pouring through her from the questions just asked of her— "Where did you go?"

She'd never told anybody her story. It was too horrific for someone to hear. But she never would forget any detail, never stop suffering the pain. It made her who she was, and besides a few things, she was proud of who she was.

Too bad her parents hadn't thought the same.

She couldn't explain it, the awe and beauty that filled her heart when she looked at Leigh Hale. Leigh was just another person, but she was perfect. Everything Marleen wanted to embody.

Marleen had done her best to keep up with all her idol did in school. Excellent grades, different sports, hanging at the popular places. Every picture she could find of Leigh and some she'd taken on her own, she tacked to her basement bedroom wall. That way she'd be able to see perfection and love whenever she wanted.

Her parents never came down to her bedroom. Her father couldn't stand the damp, musty smell that dwelled in many underground structures. She didn't mind it. After a minute, she didn't even notice it.

The two adults in the house paid her little attention as long as she went to church twice a week with them. There were no hugs, no sharing of feelings. In fact, she was afraid of her father. Any time he spoke, it was to discipline or criticize her.

She was never good enough for him. He was never proud of her. Never attended any sporting events she participated in.

The three of them seldom talked, at least, until her junior year in school. At dinner one night around the table, her mother asked why she didn't go on dates. They had many friends from church who had boys her age.

She shrugged and said none of them interested her. They were boring and talked about stupid stuff. It was dropped until her senior year when she started to rebel.

At first, it was minor things. She stopped doing homework and focused on her idol who she loved to cheer on from the shadows. The girl who made her smile just being in her presence. Her heart was light when Leigh was around.

Everyone wanted to be around Leigh. She was funny, fun, hardworking, smart. Everything that she wasn't. Her dad would've wanted Leigh for a daughter.

When Marleen started using excuses to get out of going to church, she knew her parents weren't happy, but she promised she'd go to confession to tell of her wicked sinful ways. She was eighteen years old. What the fuck could she do that was wicked and sinful? The thought of finding out appealed to her too much. But she never had the courage to truly find out.

When prom came around her senior year, she couldn't believe one of the popular guys asked her to go. She told him no. She had no desire to be around him. Then somehow her mother found out and pressured her into accepting, going as far as buying her a dress that showed her chest—not her breasts, just her upper chest.

When her date showed to pick her up, her father wanted to meet him. When the good-looking, burley boy walked into her home, her father's eyes nearly popped out of his head. He stared at her for a moment then shook the boy's hand.

He'd said to behave, and she knew exactly what he meant.

She had health class and the internet, so she understood sex and the process of having it, which she didn't see as exciting. She had no idea what the whole uproar about having sex was.

She was sure her parents did it once, her mom getting pregnant, then never again. They never kissed or held hands or said kind, loving words to each other. That was all part of loving someone, right? Wanting to be with someone all the time.

Well, Marleen wanted to be with Leigh all the time. But she went to the prom with a guy instead and hoped to see her obsession later in the night.

Her quick descent into Hell started.

She had no idea why the popular guy had asked her to the prom. Apparently, she hadn't seen any of those movies where the popular guys go out with the ugliest girl just so he can pressure her into sex. Those types of movies were never allowed in her parents' home.

They started with a shot of vodka in his car after they'd left her home. And, whoa, was that an eye-opener. It burned going down her throat. But everyone who was cool in school drank it. So she had to, also, if she wanted to hang out with them. She had no idea why her father drank so much of it. It was disgusting.

Then came another shot when they got to the prom. Her date smuggled the bottle inside and seated them back by the corner. She caught him frequently looking at the other guys and lifting his chin. They did the same and looked at her with a smile. She really thought the guys were nice and welcoming her to their "group." Well, *group* was correct, but not what she was thinking.

After several more shots, she could barely stand. Her date asked her if she wanted to walk around outside and get some fresh air. Sure, she had no problem with that, except she couldn't walk for shit. Without his arm around her waist, she'd face plant on the floor.

Outside, they wandered the parking lot toward

the back where the light was poor. She was okay with that since the bright lights hurt her eyes.

From his pocket, he pulled out a key fob and pressed a button. The back of the SUV they stood by unlocked. She was confused. This wasn't the car he drove her to the dance in. When she said that, he lifted her and set her in the rear interior.

Now she was getting scared. She tried to hop down, but her date grabbed her arm and dragged her back. When two guys in the front seats grabbed her arms, she wondered when they got there and what were they doing.

Her date shoved fabric into her mouth then slapped a piece of duct tape over that. That was when she knew she was in trouble. She tried to fight, but her head spun so much, she nearly threw up.

At that point in the story, Leigh, tear soaked, asked her to stop. She couldn't hear the rest of that night nor did she need to.

Marleen moved on to what happened later that night. The guys drove near her home and pushed her out of the SUV, where she staggered her way home. Her father flipped out, calling her a disgusting whore who needed to beg for forgiveness, or else she was going to Hell.

When she told him she hated men and preferred women for company, he slapped her, telling her she was no longer his daughter. He couldn't have such an abomination in his home. His god would punish him for housing such a sinner.

Two days later, her mother drove her with one suitcase to an aunt's four hours away. There were no goodbyes, no hugs, no words. Hell, her mother hadn't even gotten out of the car.

Her aunt wasn't that bad. The old woman was kind and loving. More of a grandmotherly type. They bonded over food and cooking. Marleen was the happiest she'd been in years.

Shortly after she turned eighteen, her aunt passed away. She called her parents, left a message, and they never called her back. Because she was considered an adult, the government had no help for her. She was homeless and penniless with nowhere to go. She walked the streets, trying to survive before a man promised her a home and food.

He forgot to mention all the men who would be fucking her day and night. A pretty, young blonde was the jackpot for traffickers. She became his prized asset with a waiting list. That was until one of the clients laid his gun on a chair. After shooting a few people, including the main man himself, she was on the run. Once again, on her own.

She got jobs in low-end restaurants to make enough money to stay alive. She avoided people, sleeping on the streets and bathing when she washed her work clothes. There were so many people on the streets, she was just a statistic.

With her long hair and looks, it wasn't long before she was approached by a man who promised her love and family. Well, the love meant she was protected from others, the family being a group of powerful gang members.

The only way to stay out of bedrooms was to make delicious food that the leader preferred over others screwing her. There, she became engrained with gang culture and met a group of females who adopted her for the most part. She shaved her hair, got piercings and tattoos to be like them.

She was also introduced to sex between females. If she had to choose, she chose the women. They didn't hurt her or hit her. In fact, they showed her the pleasure that could come from sexual gratifications—orgasms. Something she'd never experienced. From there, her life turned around.

New opportunities and doors opened due to her fresh and inventive cooking style. She moved to bigger and bigger restaurants. She saved her money and about six months ago she was close to Denali Ridge and wanted to settle in the small town. She found out her father died, and she couldn't have been happier.

Her mother, she never sought out, even though Marleen knew where she was. But the damage was done to her soul.

So many times she'd wanted to end it all, put an end to the abuse. Her acquired gun would have done the job perfectly. But one thing held her back —her father's fucking religion. It had been drilled into her that suicide would send her straight to Hell.

She tried not to believe that so she could stop the pain. But the thought of spending eternity in a worse condition than what she was in scared her too much. She welcomed death by any means but her own hand. No such luck.

She'd prayed to die. The pain inside her never went away except when she was too immersed in cooking. But the moment she saw Leigh in the restaurant that she co-owned, her heart lightened, and she felt happiness for the first time in years.

Marleen poured Leigh her fourth glass of wine which she didn't finish before falling unconscious.

CHAPTER TWENTY-FIVE

Xander walked into the hotel and headed to the office behind locked doors. Julian paced outside, talking on his phone. When he reached Julian, his second-in-command hung up.

Xander growled, "What's so important that you dragged me away from my mate?"

"I got news," he said. "Bad news."

Shit. Xander waved him into his office then sat behind his desk. "Whatcha got?"

"Our guy in New York dug deeper, hacking Barnes' system. Seems he is running a Ponzi scheme with some very rich clients. Of course, the money he's stealing has fake reports and online info. Looks very professional. He's been doing it for a while now."

Xander leaned back. "I'm sure he'd kill anyone who could tell the police. That includes girlfriends. I see why Leigh is scared for her life. She discovered what the douche bag was doing and ran." He sat forward and slammed a hand on his desk. "Damn it."

He was having second thoughts about the burglars. How long had she been in town before the two men broke in? Was it long enough for Barnes to send out assassins?

"What's going through your head, boss?" Julian asked.

"I don't want her out of my sight." He picked up his phone and dialed Harlan.

The other line picked up. "Yello."

He shook his head at Harlan's laidback personality. "Is she home?" But Xander would trust his life to the man. He'd proven his care and loyalty many times.

"Yup, and that lady chef is with her. They've been there a while visiting."

"Nothing suspicious?"

"Nope, the street is rather quiet. Only those living on it come by."

"Good."

"Boss, if she leaves, do you want me to follow her or watch the house?" Harlan asked.

Damn, that was a good question. He figured the only reason she'd leave would be because she was with him. That left the home open for others to get in.

"Watch the house. I don't want someone inside waiting for her."

"You got it." He hung up.

"What about this Barnes guy?" Julian asked.

"Leigh said the police were investigating. She'd contacted them before she left."

"Why haven't they arrested the man then?"

"Human police are slow." That was why he never depended on the locals for anything casino or hotel related.

"They can't be that slow. Our guy found stuff in less than twenty-four hours. When did your mate talk to the PD?" His second had a point.

Xander picked up his phone and scrolled through his contacts to the *F*s and tapped on his FBI contact. Xander gave the guy the lowdown and told him to get with the NYPD to see who was investigating. Something didn't smell right. Now he'd have to wait.

"Have you spoken with the women in room 109 yet?" Julian asked.

Damn, he'd almost forgotten about her. He stood from his office chair. "Let's talk with her now."

The two made their way past the hotel's check-in desk and down the hall to the rooms that no guests were given. He knocked on the door. Staci opened the door with the security chain latched.

"Is this a good time to talk?" he asked.

Staci closed the door, unhooked the chain, and opened the entry for them. "Yeah, this is good." They walked in. He noted the bruise on her cheek had faded and the scratches had scabbed over.

On the bed sat a boy about eight years old watching cartoons. "Hey," Xander said, putting his fist out.

The boy bumped his fist with his own. "Hey, Xander."

"How are you doing?" Xander asked.

"Good, the waffles are really great here. I'd never had one before." His mom looked down at him and smiled. Xander saw the family resemblance with the eyes and chins.

She said, "I contacted a shelter in Atlanta that will take us. They have basic jobs for those who want to work. They also have a person who stays with the children during the day."

"Will you be safe there?" he asked.

"I think so. I wouldn't know why my husband would ever go there to search for us."

"Good." Xander glanced at the partially open closet. "Did you get enough clothes for both of you?"

"Thank you, Xander. I did for me. The gift shop didn't have much in boys' sizes, but he doesn't change clothes often."

He nodded, pulling out his wallet. "Take this." He handed her ten $50 bills. "This should be enough to buy food and whatever else you need before you find work."

The woman covered her mouth, tears forming in her eyes. "I can't thank you enough—" A sob cut off her words. Julian reached out to hug her. Xander appreciated his partner's thoughtfulness. Now with his mate, he nor his lion wanted to have another woman in his arms even for something as innocent as a shoulder to cry on.

"Any idea when the bus leaves for Atlanta?" he asked.

Wiping her eyes, Staci pulled away from Julian. "The next one leaves in an hour."

He turned to his friend. Julian said, "As soon as you guys are ready, I'll give you a ride to the station." Yeah, they'd done this enough times that they didn't need to ask each other questions anymore.

Xander slapped his hand on Julian's shoulder as he passed. "Take them out the back so nobody identifies her. Thanks for taking them."

"Anytime, Alpha," Julian replied. "I'll see you later tonight?"

"Hopefully, tomorrow. I plan to spend the night with my mate again." With that, he left the room, headed back to the office. Once again behind his desk, he picked up the phone and dialed their Human Resources department.

"This is Karen."

"Hi, Karen. This is Xander."

"Hey, Alpha. What can I do for you?"

"I need another advance on my paycheck," he said.

"Seriously?" the woman replied. He chuckled at her pretending to be disgusted with him. "You're not going to have much of a check left if you keep this up. You know that."

He laughed. "I know. What can I say? Like my

mother always says, I burn through money like it's water."

"Well, you've worked your ass off for it so it's understandable. How much are you wanting?"

"Three hundred would be fine."

"I'll have it couriered over shortly."

"Thanks, Karen." He pulled the phone from his ear, but heard his employee's voice.

"Oh, Alpha, when do we all get to meet your mate?"

For a moment, he was speechless. How did she know about Leigh already?

"Don't worry," she said. "We all know about her. You can't keep a secret like that from getting out. When she's ready, you just let us know. Since she's human, we'll tell her *everything* she needs to know."

And, damn, if that didn't scare the living hell out of him.

Karen cackled. "Bye, Alpha."

Speaking of mate, he pulled his cell phone from his pocket and dialed up the love of his life. The phone rang several times before a voice came on the other side.

"Don't call anymore," the voice said.

"Excuse me?" He was caught so off guard, he

didn't know what to think. He pulled the phone back to see if he'd dialed the right number.

"Leigh doesn't want to see or talk to you ever again. Go away."

"Hold on one damn minute. Who is this?"

There was a pause before his answer came in a soft mutter. "Marleen."

"What are you talking about? Leigh and I care for each other. We're—"

"No. She hates you and doesn't want to see you again. Stay away, animal. She's mine." The line went silent. He redialed but nobody picked up. He needed to talk with Leigh.

What the fuck was that all about?

He called Harlan in the car stationed outside his mate's home.

"Hey...boss," Harlan replied in an unusual manner.

"Who's in my mate's home?"

"Just the chef woman who used to work at the hotel," he replied.

"Do you know her name?"

"Uh, maybe Mary or Marilyn."

"Marleen," Xander said.

"Yeah, that sounds right."

"Let me know if anything happens."

"Sure, bo—"

Xander cut off the line and picked up his desk phone, dialed the extension for HR, then drummed his fingers on the wooden top.

"This is Karen."

"Karen, Xander again."

"The guy with the money just left—"

"Thank you, but I need something else. Pull the file on a female named Marleen. She worked here a short time as a cook."

"Oh, yeah. Ms. Capple."

"Why do you say it that way?"

"She caused a little trouble by hitting on a few of the young, mated females. The mates didn't appreciate it. Even if Marleen was female."

"You're saying she is LGBT?" he asked, thoroughly confused by this whole thing.

"Q," Karen said.

"Q what?"

Karen said, "It' LGBTQ." He got the first four letter meanings—lesbian, gay, bisexual, transgender. She clarified for him. "The Q stands for questioning. And if we go for the full it's LGBTQAP."

"AP?"

"Asexual and Pansexual."

"Seriously?" He didn't know how to reply to

that. There was a whole world out there he knew very little about.

"If you're going to be politically correct, might as well get it right."

"These letters are all confusing. What happened to stuff I can remember?" he mumbled.

"That doesn't exist anymore," she answered. "It's Binary, Non-binary, and Agender."

Once again, he was left speechless. "Are you kidding me? Trying to confuse the old man of the group? 'Cause you're doing a great job of it."

Karen laughed. "No, Alpha. That's just the way of the world today. As your HR head, it's my job to know."

"You're doing a great job, Karen. Don't *ever* leave."

She chuckled. "I have Ms. Capple's file. She has a couple warnings on sexual harassment from female employees and many rave reviews from customers on her food."

"Does it list why she no longer works with us?"

"It says that she was part-time, and we chose not to extend the offer to full-time."

That wasn't much help, but he thanked her and hung up. He was beginning to think it wasn't Leigh who didn't like him, but Marleen.

His mobile phone rang. "Yeah, Harlan."

"Boss, you might want to come over here. There's a white car that might be checking out your mate's home."

Xander was up and out his office door in a heartbeat. "I'm on my way. Don't let them get in the house."

"K, boss. I'll stall them." The sound of a car door opening and closing came through the line.

Xander heard Harlan's voice as if the man had left his phone connected, but not talking into it. Much like a butt dial. "Hey, stop," he heard Harlan say. "Hey, guys, you lost? I'm Harlan. I live across the road. Say, this is a nice car. Do you need directions? I got a map in my car. You all live here in town..."

From the phone, he heard a loud pop. A gunshot? "Harlan!" he shouted. No answer. "Harlan!"

CHAPTER TWENTY-SIX

Leigh heard a voice that seemed far away. Her head thumped with an ice pick jabbing her brain. A soft touch brushed down her arm, grazing the side of her breast.

"You're so beautiful, so perfect. Your skin is as soft as it looks."

Through her pain, she tried to figure out whose voice whispered in her ear. Marleen? But that didn't make sense. Leigh was lying on her back, she guessed on her bed. Her eyes wouldn't open to let her see what was going on. What was wrong with her? Why couldn't she move.

"I've wanted to touch you for so long. You know that, right?" Marleen said. "If not for my bastard father sending me away. He could never love someone like me." Her voice ended as a heart-wrenching squeak. "I would've had you so long ago."

What did she mean by that? So long ago? In school? They barely talked. But Marleen was always there. Every class, every sport, every hang out. Oh my god. Had Marleen been obsessed with her in school?

Marleen giggled. "I had it all planned out for us. After graduation, we would've gone on a road trip, just you and me. We would've seen all the sights and spent nights in each other's arms."

Another feather-light touch caressed over her breast and down her stomach.

"My beautiful Leigh, you came back to me. I'll protect you from that beast. Don't worry about that. I won't let him hurt you." A shudder passed through her friend who she realized was pressed against her side. Skin to skin. She was naked.

Panic seized her thoughts. How did she get in bed? Why didn't she remember undressing? Last thing she recalled was Marleen making her drink the rest of her wine. Was the liquid drugged? But why would Marleen do such a thing?

"I'd rather kill you than let you suffer the endless pain he'll put you through to satisfy his cock. I'll never let that happen to you." Her voice became a whisper Leigh had to focus on to understand.

"He won't let up no matter how many times you scream at him to stop. He'll keep stabbing and stabbing, ignoring the blood until his cock throbs and puts his disgust in you." Leigh felt a kiss on her shoulder and grazing of fingers on the inside of her thigh. "Then as soon as he leaves, the next one comes in. I won't let that happen to you. I promise."

Her voice broke into sobs, her body shaking against Leigh's. What had her friend gone through to want to protect her so much? Where had she been since her father kicked her out of the house? The first thing that came to mind was human trafficking.

Marleen had long blonde hair and was very pretty. Someone a trafficker would pay, and get, a lot of money for. The gun her friend pulled out. She seemed to know how to handle it. Leigh wouldn't think a family member in another state would teach her how to use a gun. No, Marleen didn't go to live with family.

A firework popped outside the house nearby.

Her body jumped along with the woman in bed with her. Finally, Leigh could move her hands.

"What the fuck?" Marleen threw off the blankets and peeked through the curtains to the front of the house. "Who the fuck?" She grabbed her gun and ran out the bedroom door.

Leigh rolled onto her side and pushed herself to sit up. The shattering of glass was accompanied by two sets of shots ripping through her home. What was happening?

Her bedroom door slammed shut and Marleen pushed the dresser in front of it.

"Leigh, get up. Open the window. We gotta get out of here."

Leigh dragged her legs over the side of the mattress, trying to move quickly, but her body just wasn't responding. She saw her robe on the floor and was able to hook her toe under it to lift it up. As she wrapped the material around herself, Marleen was kicking out the screen from the window overlooking the driveway.

The woman hurried to her and laid a palm on the side of her face. "Look at me, Leigh," Marleen said. Her balance was there, but she could barely focus on the naked person. "There are men here with guns. I don't know why, but I'm getting you out of here. Do you understand?"

She nodded. Bullets splintered through the door, hitting the wall. Marleen returned fire, getting a cursing scream and a heavy thump outside the door. "Son of a bitch, you bitch!" came from the hall.

Leigh gasped. That voice she knew too well. William. He was here. He was going to kill her.

Marleen stared at her for a moment. "Guess you know who that is?"

She nodded and croaked out, "Ex-boyfriend."

Marleen grabbed her hand and led her to the open window. "This is how we're gonna do this, my love. I'm going out first, then I'll pull you through, okay?"

Leigh heard the words, but Marleen was moving and talking so fast, her drugged brain couldn't keep up. Next thing she knew, her world turned upside down and she thought she was going to puke. Then she was outside on the ground.

"We're going to my car—"

Leigh looked up to see what had stopped her savior and kidnapper mid-sentence. Xander ran across the street, shifting, and headed for the front of her home. She tried to holler at him, but she could barely sit up against the house.

Marleen cocked her handgun, eyes narrowed and pinned on Xander. "Don't move, honey. I'll be right back after taking out two birds with two bullets."

Leigh reached out to stop her, but her arms gave out, keeping her flat on the ground. Marleen disappeared around the corner toward the front door.

CHAPTER TWENTY-SEVEN

Xander broke a few traffic laws on his race to his mate's home. He'd do extra community service to make up for it later. He had to find out what was going on at his mate's home. When he turned down the street, he saw Harlan lying on the sidewalk, a dark puddle underneath him.

Xander slammed on the brakes and slid sideways in the street. He jumped out and ran to his guard, kneeling beside the man. His pride member's heart beat, but much too slowly and losing the tempo it had.

Blood-stained hands covered his chest. Whoever was in the car shot his man. This person would die. "Harlan, you have to shift."

"Weak," he breathed out.

Son of a bitch. Xander placed a hand on the guard's heart and forehead, summoning all the power granted to an alpha. There was no way a pride member or its animal could refuse him with an order. "Harlan, as the alpha of the Denali pride, I demand you shift now." He held his breath, waiting to see if he was too late. With a pop of snapping bone, he released the air in his lungs.

As Harlan shifted and sprouted golden fur, the metal slug fell to the concrete. The shift stitched up the damage done by the shooter; his guard should be all right. Harlan lay on his side in lion form, panting heavily.

"You going to be okay?" Xander asked. Harlan grunted which was enough for him. He got to his feet and sprinted across the yard toward his mate's house. He shifted halfway there, intent on not slowing to knock.

Reaching the porch, he launched himself into the air and body-slammed the wood barrier. It exploded in with little resistance. Hitting the floor hard, he rolled before finding his footing.

A man in his path scrambled backward and fell, screaming. Terror shined in the stranger's eyes.

Trying to get up to run, the man raised a gun and shot wildly at his lion. Xander crouched to his belly to make as small of a target as possible. He had no idea who the soon-to-be-dead chump was, but at this point, it didn't matter. He was going down.

The stench of death tickled his nose along with a human smell he didn't recognize. His mate's aroma lingered lightly, but not surrounded by the odor of blood. She was somewhere in the house, hopefully not injured. Should he search her out or take care of the guy who apparently wanted her dead?

He ended this now. His mate would never be hunted again.

While the man ran toward the kitchen, Xander listened for heartbeats in the house. He sensed one nearby. That had to be Leigh. So he padded through the house to the kitchen to see the glass broken from the opened door. He shifted and peeked out the exit to see if the man waited to shoot him coming out the door. Nobody was around.

He followed the scent of fear and body stink along the back of the house toward the driveway. When he made the corner, he saw the man had

Leigh in front of him, the gun to her head. They were backing toward the last vehicle in the drive.

How the hell did he get ahold of her?

Xander grimaced, advancing on the man. "I don't know who the fuck you are, but let her go right now."

The man stopped, a smile on his face. "You must be the one fucking my ex-girlfriend. Good lay, isn't she?" He squeezed Leigh tighter to him, edging away. "I was even thinking about keeping her, but after what she told my friend in the police department, sadly, that has to change."

"Your friend?" Xander said. Well, butter his balls and call him a biscuit. "There is no investigation, is there?" Leigh groaned, her feet dragging. She wasn't happy with that knowledge either. "So obviously, you're Barnes."

Barnes leaned his head down to his mate's ear. "You got yourself a smart one. From one rich man to another."

Leigh snorted. "Except, he's great in bed while your little dinky barely worked." She smiled at her smartass comment until Barnes slapped the handle of his gun against her head. She slumped against him, weighing him down.

Barnes grunted, trying to get a better hold on his captive.

"Just drop her," Xander said, lifting his hands. "I don't have a gun. Get in your car and drive away."

Barnes' eyes glanced at his naked body. There was no place he could hide a gun. The problem was he didn't trust that Barnes wouldn't kill Leigh before he dropped her.

The man smiled. "You really are stupid, aren't you? I can shoot her and still get to my car."

Xander shrugged. He could mention that the FBI was onto him and no matter what he did, he was going to jail. "Let her go. Do you really want to add murder to your list of crimes? You'll be in prison a hell of a lot longer if you do."

Barnes frowned. "The bitch opened her mouth to you, too. Fuck." He stared at Xander for a moment. "Guess I have to kill both of you then." He maneuvered Leigh in his arm to get her head up.

Xander charged, hoping to reach him before he killed his mate. But instincts told him he was too far away. Even shifter speed wouldn't get him there.

Barnes put the gun to his mate's head and a shot fired.

CHAPTER TWENTY-EIGHT

Leigh felt her body jerk up and her head snap back against whoever was holding her. Instinctively, she knew it wasn't Xander. He was never rough with her. A loud explosion-like sound beat her brains more than they were already and she felt herself falling backward, still in the grip of whoever had her.

Forcing her eyes open, she saw Xander running toward her. Terror filled his expression. She landed hard on a cushy surface and rolled to the side. Turning her head to the side, she saw William with a growing blood stain on his shirt lying next to the cars.

A naked Xander had her in his arms and dragging her toward the house. Who had shot William?

He knelt, letting her remain on her knees where she wrapped her hands around him. He squeezed her to him. She felt him shaking and rubbed her hands along his back.

"I almost lost you." He placed kisses on her shoulder. "God, I love you, Leigh."

"It's over. I'm okay. We're okay," she repeated, on the edge of breaking into a sob herself.

"Not yet." Marleen stood next to Xander, gun close to his ear. "I won't let him hurt you, Leigh."

"No, Marleen," Leigh's body finally found the ability to move. She jumped up from Xander's hold, fumbling a bit from her head spinning. She tugged up Marleen's hand, taking the weapon and scooting her farther from Xander. "He would never hurt me. He loves me..."

In the span of a heartbeat, memories flashed in her head. Images of the children's smiling faces when they saw Xander; the teacher's relaxed and happy ways around him; the way he looked at her with such love in his eyes at the bookstore and when he made love to her.

His tenderness and caring, concern for others, and his love for his pride proved more believable than any rumor from employees who seldom got the whole story.

She would have to deal with the things Marleen said, if they were true, which she had to doubt. But she didn't want anything keeping them apart. She didn't want to live without him.

Leigh continued her sentence. "And I love him."

"No. He can't take care of you like I can. I would never make you bleed. I won't ever hit you."

Leigh's heart broke for the horror Marleen lived through. Leigh hugged the woman. "I'm so sorry for what happened to you. I wish I could go back in time and prevent all that you suffered. If I could take your pain for you, I would."

"I don't wish my pain on anyone. There are times *I* can barely handle it. During those moments, I'd think back and remember how we were in school. You were amazing. Great grades, excelling at sports and everything you tried, everybody loving you and wanting to be with you. And I'd forget about my pain and be happy in the beauty you brought me."

Leigh didn't know what to say to such a confession. She'd never known the girl even wanted to be friends back then. But if she was able to help this woman in her arms through tough times, then it was what it was. She'd let Marleen keep the memories. But that was all she could give.

Marleen tilted up her head on Leigh's shoulder. Then the world slowed to a crawl.

Marleen pushed her to the side and twisted at the same time. When Leigh faced the opposite direction, she saw the reason for the woman's actions. Lying on the ground, William had lifted his gun, aimed at her back. Marleen turned them around so she could take the bullet for Leigh.

From between the cars, a lion charged William and tore off the arm attached to the hand with the gun.

The impact knocked them to the ground. Leigh was yelling to dial 911 before she even got up. She gently laid her life's protector on the grass.

"Hold on, Marleen. An ambulance will be here in a minute. They'll take care of you." Leigh brushed wild hair from Marleen's face.

Marleen's head rolled side to side. "I'm...sorry I...drugged...you...wine."

"It's okay," Leigh said, "I'll kick your ass when you're all better."

Her friend forced air into her lung, a wheezing sound when she exhaled. "All I said...about Xander...lies. I'm sorry. I just...wanted you to...love me."

"I do, Marleen. You saved my life, twice. Without you, my ex would've killed me."

The woman grinned. "Tell your mate...if he...ever hurts...you...I will...haunt his ass."

Leigh laughed through her rolling tears. "You can tell him yourself. Just hold on."

Marleen lifted her hand, resting her palm on Leigh's cheek. Leigh leaned into it, holding it with her own hands. Her friend's eyes moved away. "Be happy, Leigh. Love. Let him love you. Thank you for everything. Thank you for saving me."

She held Marleen's hand to her face until her own grip was the only thing keeping the touch there.

For the first time since reuniting with her abused and tormented friend, Leigh saw a true happiness and serenity on Marleen's face. The woman had found a place where they would love her unconditionally. No more pain, no more hurting.

Marleen had found her peace.

CHAPTER TWENTY-NINE

Leigh sat on the edge of Xander's bed still wrapped in the towel after her shower. Her heart ached for the loss of Marleen. It had been two days since the insanity of everything had happened, but she couldn't get over how sad Marleen's life had been. How she'd never gotten to be truly happy.

"Are you okay?" Xander asked, sitting on the bed beside her. He curled an arm around her shoulders and hugged her to his side.

Leaning her head on the curve of his neck, she gave a soft nod. "I guess."

"I'm sorry about Marleen, love. She made the ultimate sacrifice," he murmured. "I wish she was here to tell her how grateful I am for your life."

She glanced up and met his gaze. "She said something before she died. She told me to love you. To let you love me." She inhaled hard and let it out slowly. "I love you, Xander." She swallowed at the lump in her throat. "I was so scared to love you. So scared to allow myself to believe that I finally found the right man."

He moved to face her more and cupped her face in his hands. "I love you so much, Leigh. More than I can say. More than I can describe." He brushed his lips over hers in a sweet kiss. "I just hope you will let me spend my life showing you how priceless you are."

A slow smile spread over her lips. She leaned in and kissed him, giving him her lips. He already had her heart. The kiss was slow, tender and full of love. He drove his tongue deep into her mouth. The kiss switched from soft and sweet to hot and demanding. He took and gave. Oh, her body flamed instantly with his drugging lips.

Her mind was a muddled mess when she felt the towel being tugged off her body.

It took all her focus to tear her lips from the possessive and hot kiss. "Xander?"

He groaned and stood, removing his clothing in

record time. "I need you, Leigh. I want you to be my mate, love."

She gulped down the moan working up her throat. Her pussy slickened and readied for him. This blazing passion coupled with his declaration of love was absolutely perfect. It made her feel loved and turned her on like crazy. His eyes glowed bright and another rumble sounded in his chest.

"Are you ready?"

She nodded. "I am. I love you. Make me your mate. Make me yours."

His lips took hers in another deep kiss. His hunger seemed to grow with each touch. He pressed her back on the bed. His body vibrated over hers. She dug her nails into his tense arms, grasping at his smooth, fevered skin.

He slipped a hand between her legs and groaned. "Hot," he said and licked her bottom lip, nipping it between his teeth. "Wet."

Fuck, this was so good. He hadn't even done much, and her body was already wound tight. She wiggled on his finger, wanting the digit to penetrate her and calm the fire he'd ignited in her core. God. Xander and his growly voice were hot as hell.

The wild eyes. The deep growls, and the almost uncontrollable way he rubbed his body over hers was sexier than anything she'd ever experienced.

"Xander,"

"I need you, Leigh. Now. I. Can't. Wait." He caged her body. She panted, lifted her legs and curled them around his waist, gripping his arms. He met her gaze. The beast stared at her through his eyes.

Wild.

Possessive.

Demanding.

He palmed her ass and drove into her in a forceful thrust.

She gasped at the intense feeling of fullness. "Oh, god."

"Fuck," he grunted. He pounded into her pussy in quick hard drives. He took her hard, fast and she loved it. Every. Second.

One more thing she learned about herself. She liked wild sex. She sure as hell enjoyed the hot, hard slide of his cock slamming into her and pressing her into the mattress. The sound of the banging headboard on the wall was music to her ears.

He sucked on her neck, drawing circles on her

flesh and growling with each drive. Her orgasm took her by surprise with its speed. A burning wave of pleasure sucked her under and hurled her out into space.

Her body shook, and he kissed her at the same time she screamed, drinking in her breathless call of his name. Her sex tightened around his cock and flutters of mini orgasms proceeded to flare shockwaves through her channel.

Their breaths co-mingled. He growled into their kiss. Deep. So deep the rumble felt as if it were coming out of her chest. Then she was on her stomach, knees to chest and upper body flush on the bed. He drove deep, thrusting fast and hard. With every push into her sex, she felt he grew bigger, hotter inside her.

"Mine!" He growled.

"Yes!"

"I'm going to come inside you, Leigh," he whispered by her ear. "I'm going to fill you up with my cum."

"Yes, Xander. Yes, please."

"You could get pregnant with my offspring."

She grunted. "Give me all your babies. I love you."

Another rumble sounded from him. "Fuck, love. I'm going to do just that. Are you sure?"

"Positive," she shuddered. "I want you and our family."

One deep drive and he tensed. Another and he shook. On the third, he roared loud, biting the back of her shoulder and scratching her hips with his nails as he gripped her tight. One final drive and he stopped, his cock pulsing and filling her with his heated seed.

She panted as they fell on the bed sideways, with him still inside her. He kissed her shoulder and up her neck. "I love you so much, Leigh. My mate."

She let out a sharp breath and cuddled into him. "I love you, too."

"Now we just need to get married. Cover all the bases."

A smile spread over her lips. She thought of Balgair, Parker and Jade and how right they'd been. Xander loved her. Her heart was full of happiness. *I'm going to be happy, Marleen. For both of us.*

He kissed her shoulder, up to her ear, and licked her earlobe. Then he pulled out of her slowly. She almost whimpered from the loss of heat.

“I’m going to make you happy, Leigh. I promise.”

She believed him.

EPILOGUE

Xander opened the door to the little bookstore, the tinkling bell sounding overhead. On the door was a sign with the store's new name—Leigh's Books and More. He smiled to himself, so proud of what his mate had accomplished in the past weeks. Leigh was a wonder. He was lucky to have her. Lucky that she loved him as much as he loved her.

She was stronger than anyone he knew, including himself.

The kids scattered around on the floor jumped up when seeing him. "Alpha, Alpha," they all hollered, wanting to be one of those he hugged. He made sure to cuddle all of them, so no one felt left out.

"Hey, everyone," his mate called out, "be sure to put your colored pencils in the right bins. Don't forget your coloring project."

Standing to the side, he watched as the kids scurried around like a colony of ants, gathering papers and backpacks, hollering bye to his mate.

"Oh," Leigh said, "next week we're painting. Bring an old shirt."

As the room emptied, he made his way to the sexiest woman in the building. He whispered into her hear, "Do you know how hot you look being in charge."

Leigh grinned and whispered, "Are you saying I get to tie you up tonight?" He backed her against a shelf. "Love, you can tie me up anytime you want." A growl started deep in his chest.

"Bye, Alpha, Ms. Leigh." The last of the little ones walked out with his mother.

"We're all alone, Ms. Leigh. Would you like to play bookstore owner and sexy shopper?"

She put her arms around his neck. "Hmm. Who would be the sexy shopper?" She gave him a peck on the lips. "Let me lock up and we can go out back."

"Good. I have some good news to share with you." He watched her as she moved through the store, the sway of her hips, the sleek line of her neck and shoulders. Everything about her turned him on. She took his hand and guided him through the rear door.

He loved this area since they discovered it after Leigh used the money returned to her from Barnes's illegal scheme to buy the store. It was the perfect private nook with an overhead trellis intertwined with ivy and a wooden swing.

He sat, pulling her onto his lap, and rocked them gently.

"What's this good news you have to share?" she asked.

"The pride council approved the plans for the women's shelter," he said. Leigh gasped and threw her hands around him in a big hug.

"Thank you, thank you, thank you. When do we break ground?" He loved her eagerness to help others needing a place to stay.

"First, love, we need to have plans for a building." He chuckled.

"Oh, that? That's easy for you. Just build something smaller than your hotels."

Xander laughed. "It's not quite that easy, but it won't take long."

"I have the perfect name—Marleen Capple

Women's Shelter," she said. This didn't surprise him. His mate would take a sad ending and turn it into something good. Why he hadn't thought of building a safe place himself boggled his mind.

"Maybe if Marleen would've had a place to go, her life might've turned out differently."

"You are amazing, my love," he said, pulling her against his chest.

"Not really. Marleen was truly amazing. All that she went through and suffered reminded me that no matter how bad I thought I had it, someone else had it much worse. She brought me something that I'd lost in the city."

"What's that?" he asked.

"Unconditional love."

His hand vibrated on her ass. She pulled out her phone and glanced at the screen. "It's Kellan." She tapped the screen and held it between them. "Hey, big brother. What's up?"

"I'm getting ready to board a plane that will get me to Denali Ridge."

His mate's face lit up. "Seriously?"

"Yeah, but a need a ride home. I was hoping you could come get me."

"Absolutely, Xander and I will be there. How

long do you plan on staying? Can we do dinner at least once?"

He heard a chuckle from one of his best friends. "I think that will work. But I'm going to be very busy while I'm there."

His mate looked at him with a questioning expression. She lifted her phone closer to herself. "Why would you be so busy here? Denali Ridge really isn't a hot spot for special ops."

Kellan laughed again. "Well, it seems that my home I'm going to live in has need of a few renovations. Like a new front door..."

Xander smiled. "That would be my bad. Well, my lion's."

Kellan continued. "Bullet holes in the walls..."

Leigh rolled her eyes. "We patched all—wait. Did you say you're going to live in?"

"Yeah," his mate's brother said, "I think it's time to come home and settle down. See family and do some catching up." Leigh dropped her phone onto his lap as she slapped hands over her mouth, tears forming in her eyes.

"Hey, man," Xander said, "it'll be good to have you back. I have just the job for someone with your skills. If you want to work that is."

"Yeah, man. Something thrilling and

dangerous?"

He laughed. "More than you've ever experienced. I have a feeling these women you'll be guarding will keep you on your toes."

"Women?" Kellan said. "How many are we talking? Would I prefer to be in a gun battle?"

Xander heard the fear in his friend's voice and laughed. "Nah, man. We'll talk when you get here." They exchanged information for the flight and said goodbye.

"I can't believe he's coming home," Leigh said, snuggling into him. "We have a lot of time to make up for."

"Speaking of time, my contact in New York called today. Said they were finally able to arrest Barnes. The last of the forensic accounting came in and combined with the photos you took of the accounts, put him guiltier than hell."

"I'm so glad," she said. "When they sell all the expensive stuff he has, I'm sure they'll have enough money to make all the clients whole. I can't believe I sent so many his way. I was so stupid."

"Hey," he adjusted his mate on his lap to see her face, "you did the right thing as soon as you found out. That's all that matters. Oh, the detective on the police force who was Barnes' friend, he's been fired, and the DA is considering prosecuting if they find anything else on him."

"Is this really the end of it all?" she said, hope in her voice. "Is it over?"

He shook his head. "No. There's one more thing to take care of." He set her on the swing beside him, then slid down on one knee. The shock on his mate's face was priceless. She was priceless.

"Leigh Hale, I've loved you since I first laid eyes on you as a child. I didn't know you were destined to be mine. But you knew what you were doing when you asked me to marry you back then." He pulled a diamond ring from his pocket. "This time, I'm asking you to marry me."

She slammed into him so hard with a hug, they nearly fell over. Good thing he was a shifter.

"Yes," she said, "I will love you forever."

The End

But wait! Keep reading for a preview of
Caught by the Wolves
Taken by the Tiger
and Chosen by the Bear

ABOUT THE AUTHOR

New York Times and USA Today Bestselling Author

Hi! I'm Milly Taiden. I love to write sexy stories featuring fun, sassy heroines with curves and growly alpha males with fur. My books are a great way to satisfy your craving for paranormal romance with action, humor, suspense and happily ever afters.

I live in Florida with my hubby, our son, and our fur babies: Speedy, Stormy and Teddy. I have a serious addiction to chocolate and cake.

I love to meet new readers, so come sign up for my newsletter and check out my Facebook page. We always have lots of fun stuff going on there.

SIGN UP FOR MILLY'S NEWSLETTER FOR LATEST NEWS!

http://eepurl.com/pt9q1

Find out more about Milly here:

www.millytaiden.com

milly@millytaiden.com

ALSO BY MILLY TAIDEN

Find out more about Milly Taiden here:

Email: millytaiden@gmail.com

Website: http://www.millytaiden.com

Facebook: http://www.facebook.com/millytaidenpage

Twitter: https://www.twitter.com/millytaiden

Printed in Great Britain
by Amazon

71719320R00154